Ida Early
Comes over the
Mountain

ALSO BY ROBERT BURCH

D. J.'s Worst Enemy

*Hut School and the
Wartime Home-Front Heroes*

Queenie Peavy

Skinny

Two That Were Tough

Wilkin's Ghost

Christmas with Ida Early

King Kong and Other Poets

Ida Early Comes over the Mountain

Robert Burch

Cover illustration by Richard Williams

SCHOLASTIC INC.
New York Toronto London Auckland Sydney

ISBN 0-590-43950-2

12 11 10 9 8 7 6 5 4 3 2 1   0 1 2 3 4 5/9

Printed in the U.S.A.   40

First Scholastic printing, October 1990

For two great-nieces
Caroline Jones
and
Mary Alice Grove

———————————

Contents

Contents

Ida Early Comes over the Mountain

"Taller than Anybody"

Ida Early came over the mountains. Or else she came around them. Randall Sutton never was sure which. He just knew that early one Saturday morning in mid-July someone had rapped on the door, and when he opened it, there she stood.

"Howdy-do?" she said, flinging out her arms as if she expected him to rush into them. She looked for all the world like a telephone pole and seemed almost as tall. At the same time she reminded him of someone, but he couldn't remember who. Her face was plain, her complexion ruddy, and her hair light brown and stringy. She was not a real young person; Randall could tell that she was well out of her teens. Nor was she old, certainly not as old as his father, who was thirty-four. She wore a patchwork shirt, a baggy brown sweater, and overalls. The elbows of the sweater and the knees of the overalls had been reinforced with scraps of canvas. Her shoes were brogans—clodhoppers, they were called—and a small buckeye dangled from one of the laces. A buckeye was said to bring good luck.

Randall didn't say anything, and his father, who had followed him to the door, only nodded. Ida Early stood there grinning. At the outset of the Depression, people had stopped occasionally to ask for a handout—food or old clothes. But times were a little better now, and there were seldom beggars at the door. And none of them ever stood grinning as if awaiting a special welcome. Finally Mr. Sutton asked, "Is there anything we can do for you?"

"Let me think," she said, brushing away a corn shuck from above her left ear. Then Randall knew who she reminded him of: she favored the scarecrow that he and his friend, J. C., had built last summer to keep birds out of the cantaloupe patch.

That was it: she looked more like a scarecrow than a telephone pole.

After Ida had scratched her head, she smiled at Mr. Sutton. "If you insist on doing something for me," she said, "you could maybe offer me a job."

Mr. Sutton smiled back at her. "Are you a lumberjack or a field hand?"

"Well," said Ida Early, "which would you be a-needing?"

"Neither. But it could be that we're wanting some help with the cooking and other chores around here."

"Well, then," said Ida, "this is your lucky day!" She waved Mr. Sutton and Randall aside so that she could enter. "I'm one of the best cooks in the Blue Ridges." The Suttons lived at the edge of the Blue Ridge Mountains—on the Georgia side—but Randall had never heard anybody speak of them as anything except "the mountains." Ida Early said, "Yes, siree, I'm one of the best cooks I know about. As a matter of fact, I'm noted in Georgia, Tennessee, and both Carolinas for my cooking."

Mr. Sutton said, "I'll have to see."

Ida looked around the hallway. "What have you got that you want cooked up?" she asked, rubbing her hands together. "Just let me at it!"

"I mean I'll have to see what Earnestine thinks."

"Is she your wife?"

"No, my sister. My wife died in spring."

"I'm sorry," said Ida. "I'm genuinely sorry. Is your sister looking after the family?"

Randall thought that "bossing the family" would be a better way of putting what Aunt Earnestine did.

"Yes," said his father, "but she's anxious to get back to her home in Atlanta. Let's talk to her." He led the way into the big room that was called the kitchen but was the dining and sitting room as well. There was a cookstove, cupboard, and icebox on one side, a table and chairs in the middle, and benches and more chairs over by the hearth.

When Mr. Sutton led Ida Early into the kitchen, Randall's sister and his twin brothers were still at the table, finishing their breakfast.

"Howdy, one and all!" said Ida, bowing to the three children.

"Good morning," said Ellen. The twins, Clay and Dewey, didn't say anything. They just stared. Ellen, being twelve, tried not to look too directly at Ida, but the twins, who were only five, seemed unable to look anywhere else. Randall's father went in search of Aunt Earnestine, leaving Ida standing in the middle of the room.

The twins, wiry and blond like all the Suttons and a bit small for their age, were identical except for a tiny scar on Dewey's forehead, the result of a fight they'd had on their second birthday. Clay had hit him with the dasher from the ice cream freezer.

Clay slid down from his chair at the table and, followed by Dewey, circled around Ida, looking up at her. One time was not enough, and they circled around her again before sitting down on a bench near the fireplace. "You're tall," said Dewey, pleasantly. "I'll bet you're taller than anybody."

Ida lifted her shoulders. "Oh, I'm not so tall. I'm as near six feet as I am seven."

"Are you a man or a woman?" asked Clay.

"Why, Clay Sutton!" said Ellen, coming away from the table. "That's not a nice thing to ask. And, anyway, can't you see she has long hair?"

"It's not *very* long," said Clay, always one to argue. "And, besides, she's got on overalls." He sounded as if that meant she must surely be a man.

"I had a dress once," said Ida Early, smiling down at the twins. "But it wasn't very practical for a lion tamer, so I switched to overalls."

Dewey was asking, "Were you really a lion tamer?" when Mr. Sutton and Aunt Earnestine came into the room. Randall always thought of Aunt Earnestine as a battleship. She wasn't especially big, but she always looked as if she were ready for war. And she moved as if everybody should get out of the way. Randall always did; he considered himself a rowboat by comparison. Before Aunt Earnestine spoke to Ida Early, she ordered Ellen and Randall to get busy clearing the breakfast dishes from the table.

Randall didn't mind doing the work, but he hated the way Aunt Earnestine ordered him and Ellen about. He hoped the woman, Ida, would be hired and Aunt Earnestine would go back to Atlanta.

The grown-ups stood across the room, talking. Mr. Sutton explained that he was foreman of a lumberyard and had to work long hours. He didn't have as much time to spend with his children as he'd like—this was the first Saturday he'd had off in a long time—and he needed someone to look after them. Soon it had been decided that Ida would be given a job. "I can't pay much," said Mr. Sutton, "on account of times are still not good, even if we do keep hearing that the Depression is easing up."

"I don't worry about the pay," said Ida, "if the job's interesting and there's plenty of work to do."

Aunt Earnestine said crossly, "There's plenty of work. You can start by cleaning the house."

Mr. Sutton said, "Maybe she'd like to sit down

for a few minutes first and get acquainted with the children."

"She can get acquainted with them while she cleans the house," said Aunt Earnestine.

Ida Early stood back of one of the big rocking chairs. "Maybe I'll just rock a few minutes first," she said, taking off the baggy sweater that she wore. Then she held the sweater over her head, twirled it around twice, and let it go. It sailed to the corner, landing neatly on the hatrack.

Everyone laughed except Aunt Earnestine, who was horrified. "We *take* our garments across the room to hang them up!" she scolded.

"Of course you do!" said Ida. "It's not just everybody who can throw things and make 'em land in exactly the right spot." Then she grinned. "But I'll be happy to teach all of you the trick to it if I could have my sweater back." Dewey raced to get it for her.

Ida sat down in the rocker. "The secret of my good aim's in the wrist movement," she said. Then she announced, "And now, ladies and gentlemen, from a sitting position!" Before Aunt Earnestine could protest, Ida took the sweater, whirled it around, and threw it to the hatrack again. She told Aunt Earnestine with a little smile, "Think how many steps you could save in a day!"

This time Clay started for the sweater, but Aunt Earnestine made him sit down.

Ida Early then unbuttoned the big pocket across the top of her overalls and brought out a nickel bag of Bull Durham tobacco. As everyone watched, she rolled a cigarette, using only one hand. Then she got up, struck a match on the seat of her overalls, and sat back down. After she had lit the cigarette and flicked the match halfway across the room into the fireplace, she dangled the bag of Bull Durham by the strings. "Anybody care for a smoke?" she asked.

Randall laughed, and she tossed the bag of tobacco to him. "Roll yourself one," she said.

"Why, Randall is only eleven years old," said Aunt Earnestine. "What do you mean by offering him a cigarette?"

"I wasn't really going to let him smoke, ma'am," said Ida. "If he had started to light up, I was going to tell him about what cigarettes have done to me." She paused, and when nobody asked what cigarettes had done to her, she told her story anyway. "You see, before I started smoking I was a splendid-looking sight."

"Were you really?" asked Dewey.

"I was indeed. I had blond curly hair, diamond rings on every finger, and dimples. I wish you could have seen me." She took a long drag on her cigarette. "But then I took to smoking, and everything changed. My hair turned stringy, just like it is now." She ran her fingers through it, and Randall thought of the coarse binder twine that he and J. C. had used in making the scarecrow's hair.

"What happened to your diamond rings?" asked Clay.

"They fell off," said Ida Early. "One by one they fell off, but I didn't mind too much. The hair doesn't bother me either, but I sure do hate it about the dimples." She looked down at Dewey and Clay, who were looking up at her, and winked at Randall and Ellen. "There's nothing nicer than a good smile," she said, "dimples or not. Nothing pleases me more."

She looked around and must have been very pleased, Randall thought, because everyone was smiling. Everyone but Aunt Earnestine.

The Stew-Making Fool

"We'll be back before noon," said Aunt Earnestine a while later. "Do you think you can look after things here?"

"Oh, yes, ma'am," answered Ida Early. "It would pleasure me to look after things."

"We'll have stew for lunch," said Aunt Earnestine. "Do you think you could prepare it?"

Ida licked her lips and said enthusiastically, "Why, I'm a stew-making fool!"

But Aunt Earnestine frowned. "The beef is cut

up and in the icebox. Brown it in the skillet before you put it in the pot to simmer. And you'll find vegetables in the pantry when it's time to add them."

Ida nodded.

"And just warm up the cornbread left from yesterday. Also, there's a bowl of turnip greens in the cupboard that can be heated."

Aunt Earnestine went ahead to the car, and Mr. Sutton asked, "Who wants candy from town?" Randall and the others scrambled to find their money. Each one had a special place for savings. Randall ran to the shoe box in the hall closet where he kept his in an empty snuff can. The rest of the box was where he stored his mitt and softball and the Indian arrowhead he'd found in the woods the day he had seen a bear. There was not much money in the snuff can, and he decided to spend only three pennies. He and Ellen were saving for Monopoly, a board game their friends had told them about. When he got back to the kitchen, Ellen was placing her order. She wanted licorice sticks; Ellen always wanted licorice sticks.

The twins wanted jawbreakers, the two-for-a-penny kind. Dewey wanted a green one and a yellow one, and Clay wanted two red ones. Randall handed his father his money, but before he could tell what he wanted, Clay was back, saying, "I believe I'll have a green one and a yellow one instead."

"Instead of two red ones," said Mr. Sutton cheerily. "I'll bring them to you: one green jaw-breaker and one yellow jawbreaker."

Randall ordered Baby Ruths, the penny ones, and Mr. Sutton said, "Now, that gets everyone, doesn't it?" But Clay was back again. "I think I want a red one instead of the green one," he said.

"And I want a red one too," said Dewey.

"Wait a minute!" said Mr. Sutton. "I'm all confused."

"Could I be of help?" asked Ida.

Mr. Sutton laughed. "I don't know, but you can try!"

Ida turned to Dewey. "Do you want a red one instead of a green one?"

"No, instead of a yellow one," said Dewey.

Ida turned back to Mr. Sutton. "That'll be a green one and a red one for Dewey and a red one and a yellow one for Clay."

"That's right!" said Dewey.

Mr. Sutton said, "Thanks, Ida. Thanks for the help."

"Don't mention it," said Ida. She winked at the twins. "Of course, the purple ones are nice too. They're grape-flavored."

Mr. Sutton grabbed his hat from the rack by the

door. "Oh, no! No more mind-changing today!" He laughed as he hurried from the room.

Randall was glad to hear his father sound happy. No one in the family had laughed much in recent months. They mourned for Mrs. Sutton. The children spoke of their mother sometimes but not as often as they had for a time. Randall supposed it had taken them a while to fully realize that nothing they could say would bring her back. He thought of her every day, and he expected everyone else did too. The twins still cried some nights because she wasn't there to put them to bed.

The Tiddlywinks Champion
of the Whole Wide World

After the car had driven away, Ida glanced at a tiddlywinks board on a shelf near the fireplace and said, "I don't suppose any of you would ever have guessed that once I was tiddlywinks champion of the whole wide world."

"I would," said Dewey. "I would have guessed it," and Clay said, "We like to play tiddlywinks."

"Do you really?" asked Ida. "Well, that's a happy fact to know! Why don't we just play a game of it right now?"

She sat down cross-legged in the middle of the room and the twins brought over the disks and the board, with its tiny cup in the center. While they were sorting the button-like disks according to color, Ida Early said, "Now let's see, do twins play separately, or should we add their scores together?"

Clay and Dewey looked at her as if they thought she was crazy.

"I mean, wouldn't it be fair for anyone under the age of six to team up? Shouldn't the rest of us be willing to combine their scores?"

"Never!" said Randall. "Not unless you combine ours." He and Ellen spent a lot of their spare time trying to beat the twins at tiddlywinks. Occasionally one of them came out ahead of Clay, but no one had ever beaten Dewey. Randall had decided that either the twins had some special built-in talent for the game or else all the hours they had played it by themselves while he and Ellen were in school had turned them into near-perfect scorers.

Ellen asked Ida, "Are we going to begin a game before you start the stew?"

"Oh, that's right," said Ida, "the stew! I know what, why don't we take turns playing and cooking? Since you're the one who remembered the stew, I wouldn't feel right about not letting you begin it. Maybe you could find that meat and brown it in a little butter." Ellen looked as if she were about to object to being left out of the first game until Ida added, "Unless you think you might not be quite old enough to shoulder such a responsibility."

"I'm twelve," said Ellen. She went across to the icebox and took out the beef that Aunt Earnestine had cut up.

Dewey said, "You're company, Ida. You get to go first."

"Thank you kindly," she said, and pressed down on one of the yellow disks that had been given her. It landed on the windowsill. Everyone laughed, and Ida acted upset. "We should have had a warm-up period!" she said. "We champion tiddly-winks players always have a warm-up period. But never mind, I'll catch up."

Randall played next, and his disk landed at the edge of the small board. "Better than the window-sill!" he said.

Clay was next, and when he snapped his disk he said, "Gingerbread!" The twins had picked up that idea from their father. He had told them that their aim would be more accurate if they thought of something pleasant while taking it. They themselves had decided that it might be even better if they said their "pleasant thought" aloud. Clay's disk landed on the board in the ring nearest the cup, scoring fifteen points for him.

Ida said, "Good for you!"

Dewey took the last turn. "Peanut butter!" he said softly as he snapped the disk. It landed with a *plink* in the tiny cup.

"Wow!" said Ida. "What luck!" Clay and Randall did not say anything; they might have said "Wow!" if Dewey had missed.

Ida landed her next disk within a few inches of the cup, and after two more turns she announced she would try Clay's and Dewey's system of having pleasant thoughts. She took careful aim and said loudly, "Feather bed!" She pressed down on the disk. It flew out the window.

"I shouldn't have thought of anything so fancy," she said. "It serves me right that the shot went wild." On her next try she shouted, "Straw mattress!" and the disk went into the cup. "See," she said, "didn't I tell you that it's best to be practical?"

Dewey won the game and Clay came in second. Ida was third. "Randall, you're the loser," said Ida. "I guess that means Ellen gets to take your place." She called across the room, "How's the stew coming?"

"It's bubbling already."

"Fine!" said Ida. "You come join in this tiddlywinks game so Randall can have his chance to help over there." Before Randall could argue she turned to him. "You wouldn't mind finding a few potatoes, would you?" As he walked toward the pantry, she added, "Peel 'em clean and throw 'em in the pot!"

The next game was played while Randall peeled potatoes. Ellen was the loser, and Ida convinced her that she was to be treated to a rare opportunity: she could look for onions and carrots and put them in the stew. Randall was invited into the tiddlywinks game again.

Ida lost the next game, and she said, "It's probably my elbow that's holding me back. It hasn't been the same since I fell off a bucking mustang."

"What's a mustang?" asked Clay.

"A horse," said Randall.

"Did you really fall off one that was jumping up and down?" asked Dewey, and Clay said, "Tell us about it."

"It's too terrible to discuss," said Ida with a shudder. "Let's play tiddlywinks." She snapped down on one of the disks.

"Hey!" said Ellen, awaiting her turn to get back into the game. "You lost! It's my turn to play."

"That's right," said Ida, "and it must be my turn to cook. But it wouldn't be fair if you weren't allowed to season the stew, now would it? After all, you started the pot to perking."

A few minutes later Ellen was at the stove, putting salt and pepper in the stew, and when it was almost done, Randall was sent to see if the meat was tender. "Stick a fork in a chunk of it," called Ida, who had sat cross-legged on the floor all morning. "And while you're on your feet, see if you can locate those greens your aunt was talking about. Heat 'em in a boiler, and you might put the cornbread in the oven while you're at it. It'll soon be time to eat."

At noon Dewey remained champion tiddlywinks player. Ida Early had been second once, and Clay had been runner-up the other times. When the last game ended, Dewey said, "All right, everybody, pay up!" That was something else he had learned from his father. Mr. Sutton always said, "Pay up!" whenever he happened to win a game—as if a bet had been placed on it.

"I'll pay you with a handshake," said Ellen, reaching across and pumping Dewey's hand up and down.

"I'll give you a love lick," said Ida, making a fist and giving Dewey a light tap on one arm.

"I'll give you a lick to grow on," said Randall, punching him on the other arm.

Dewey was laughing at the attention he was getting until Clay said, "And I'll give you a bite." He leaned over and bit his brother on the leg.

Dewey screamed, and he and Clay started fighting. Ellen and Randall yelled at the twins to stop. The noise was at its loudest when Mr. Sutton and Aunt Earnestine arrived home.

Finally everyone quieted down, and Aunt Earnestine said huffily, "I certainly hope the children haven't been carrying on like this all morning."

"No, ma'am," said Ida Early, winking at Randall. "I don't think they have. But to tell you the truth, I've been so busy cooking I've hardly had time to notice."

Bedding Down

At supper there were vegetables from the garden and warmed-over stew. "Worthy of a king!" said Mr. Sutton. "Too bad we don't know any kings or we'd invite them for a meal sometime!"

"Who'd you see in town today?" asked Randall.

"Don't believe I saw any of your friends," said his father, "but I spoke to one of the Ragsdale boys when I stopped at the filling station."

Ellen put down the ear of boiled corn that she was eating. "Marcus?" she said. "Was it Marcus?"

"The redheaded one," said Mr. Sutton, helping his plate to another serving of butter beans. "He asked how everybody was getting along out here."

"What'd you tell him?"

Mr. Sutton laughed. "I told him everybody was fine." He paused and added, "I told him *everybody* had missed seeing friends since school let out."

Ellen blushed, and Clay said, "Ellen's got a sweetheart!"

"Hush up and eat your supper!" said Aunt Earnestine. "Ellen's too young to be interested in boys."

Ellen frowned, and Mr. Sutton said, "Oh, I don't know, Earnestine. Mountain children grow up fast."

Dewey turned to Ida Early. "Did you know Ellen has a sweetheart?"

"Of course I did. Anybody as pleasant as Ellen probably has several sweethearts."

"Marcus thinks I'm pretty," said Ellen.

"Of course you are!" said Ida. "But being pleasant is a heap more important than being pretty. That's why I named it first."

"You're pleasant," said Dewey.

"Why, thank you."

Dewey added, "You're pleasanter than you are pretty." Everyone laughed.

Clay said, "Ida Early's not pretty."

Randall wondered what Ida would say. With one hand she dabbed at her face as if she were powdering it, and with the other one she pretended to fluff her hair. "You've never seen me fixed up!" she said.

The idea of Ida spruced up struck everyone as funny, including Ida herself. Randall noticed that she laughed more than anybody else.

After supper Mr. Sutton unfolded his newspaper. He handed the second section of it to the twins, who spread it out on one side of the table. They flipped pages until they came to the comic strips. Ellen glanced over their shoulders at a cartoon at the top of the page, and Clay said, "Read us the funnies!" Dewey added, "Please!"

"Later," said Ellen. "I have to finish clearing the table." The twins had pushed bowls and platters aside to make room for the paper.

"Randall, you read 'em to us, okay?" said Dewey.

"Later," said Randall. "I have to help Ellen." He didn't want to risk a lecture from Aunt Earnestine by failing to get on with the work. His aunt was in her room now, but she always came back to see that nobody was resting on the job.

"I'll read you the funnies," said Ida Early. She put a dish of candied yams into the cupboard and went over to the table. "Make some room!" Clay and Dewey slid their chairs apart and were moving one into place for Ida when Aunt Earnestine came back.

Dewey said happily, "Guess what, Aunt Earnestine? Ida Early's gonna read us the funny papers!"

"No, she's not! Ida's going to wash the dishes." Aunt Earnestine sounded very sure of it.

"Of course I am," said Ida, sitting down between Clay and Dewey. "But first we'll just have a look at Little Orphan Annie."

"Oh, boy!" said Dewey. "We like Little Orphan Annie."

After Ida had read the strip to them, Clay said, "We like Dick Tracy too."

"Well, ain't that a jolly coincidence?" said Ida. "So do I! In fact, I like 'em all!"

"So do we!" said Clay. "Let's read some more."

Ida started reading Dick Tracy to them, but Aunt Earnestine interrupted. "The comic strips will wait; the dishes won't."

"Oh, no, ma'am," said Ida. "It's the other way around. If the funnies are not read they're liable to disappear—somebody'll throw 'em out or burn them up or something. But dirty dishes? Why, I ain't never known of one of them to get away." She continued to read to the twins while Randall and Ellen washed and dried the dishes. They were accustomed to doing them, anyway, and they seemed to go faster this time because they listened to Ida.

Aunt Earnestine sat down, folded her hands in her lap, and looked as if she were about to explode. Randall and Ellen glanced over their shoulders at her and then looked at each other. They tried not to laugh.

When the twins became sleepy, Ida put them to bed and sang to them. Randall listened from the kitchen; it was the first time he had ever heard a lullaby that included yodeling. It was "Hush, Little Baby," which he'd heard often but not quite the way it was being sung now:

> *"Hush, Clay and Dewey, don't say a word,*
> *Ida's gonna buy you a mockingbird.*
> *Yodle-li-de-lady, Yodle-li-de-lady,*
> *Yodle-li-de-lady-oh!"*

There were a lot of verses, and Ida yodeled a bit after each one. After "If that looking glass gets broke, Ida's gonna buy you a billy goat," she bleated a few times like a goat. "Baa! Baa! Baa!"

When Ida returned to the kitchen, Aunt Earnestine said, "That'll be all for today. You can go ahead home."

"I'm home," said Ida.

"You're what?"

"I live here. Didn't you hire me?"

Aunt Earnestine's mouth flew open, but she didn't say anything.

Mr. Sutton put down the paper. "What's this?" he asked.

Pointing to Ida, Aunt Earnestine said, "She says she lives here."

Mr. Sutton said, "Why, Ida, I didn't know you wanted to live with us. We don't have an extra bed just now."

"Oh, I didn't mean I'd sleep in the house. Thank you, anyway, but a feed room in the barn is more my style."

"Certainly not!" said Aunt Earnestine.

"It's ideal," insisted Ida. "I like the privacy." She looked at Mr. Sutton. "The cottonseed hulls make a soft bed, and all those empty feed sacks are fine cover. One of 'em puffed up with corn shucks makes a dandy pillow." She rushed on before Aunt Earnestine could protest. "To tell the truth, I slept there last night. I got here late, so I took the liberty of accepting your hospitality before you'd even offered it."

Randall smiled. He remembered the corn shuck that had fallen to the floor when she arrived.

At last, and over Aunt Earnestine's objections, Mr. Sutton consented for Ida to sleep in one of the feed rooms. But he insisted that she take along a heavy blanket and a quilt from the house.

Ida slung the covers over one shoulder. Standing at the back door, she looked at Aunt Earnestine. "If you don't mind," she said with that same little smile, "would you send somebody to wake me when breakfast is ready?"

"When breakfast is ready?" said Aunt Earnestine crossly. Randall knew she was thinking Ida should get up and help cook it.

"Yes, ma'am," said Ida. "I'll come to the house in time to eat. I wouldn't expect you to send me a tray, but I appreciate your thoughtfulness, anyway." She closed the door and went out into the night.

"Fresh as a Ragweed"

When Randall woke up the next morning, the twins were in bed with him. Their bed was across the room, but whenever one of them had a bad dream he always woke the other and the two of them would run crawl in bed with someone else. Usually it was Randall because he was the nearest, but the other Suttons never knew when they might wake up and find the twins snuggled up to them.

Randall put his arms over his head and

stretched. Although it was midsummer, mountain nights were cool. He put his arms back under the cover and looked out at the sun that was beginning to rise. It appeared to be peeking at him from between two mountains in the distance. He stretched again and got out of bed, tucking the blanket back around the twins.

It was Randall's job to make a fire in the cookstove every morning before he went about his other chores. His next job was to draw a bucket of fresh water and bring it into the house. Then he would go to the barn to feed the livestock and do the milking. But on this morning, before he had finished dressing, he smelled smoke. The house is on fire! was his first thought. He dashed from the bedroom, pulling on his shirt as he ran. When he reached the kitchen, Ida was there, adjusting the damper on the stove. "Oh," said Randall, "it's you."

"I slept so good," said Ida, "bedded down in those nice, soft cottonseed hulls, that I woke up at dawn, fresh as a ragweed. And I decided I'd just as well be up and active."

She looked fresher than the day before, thought Randall. Instead of the patchwork shirt she wore a clean white one with her overalls. The cuffs had been cut off, and the collar was frayed. Buttons were missing, and the shirt was held together with a big safety pin. A tiny basket carved from a peach seed dangled from the pin. Randall thought of the time he'd tried to carve a basket from a peach seed. The knife had slipped, and he'd almost cut off his thumb.

Ida opened a cupboard door and asked, "Where do you keep the bacon?"

Randall went into the pantry and brought out a big slab of the home-cured meat. Ida began slicing thin strips from it. "I'll go draw some water," said Randall, reaching for the bucket that was kept on a low table near the door. Usually the bucket was almost empty in the morning, but now it was full.

"I brought in a fresh supply," said Ida.

"Thank you," said Randall, starting out the door. "Thanks a lot."

Outside, he stopped at the pigsty to give Mayflower, the sow, her breakfast—a gallon of buttermilk left from yesterday's churning. Mayflower was asleep in the corner of the pen, but the moment she heard Randall she dashed toward him. "Okay, okay!" he said, leaning over the board fence and pouring the buttermilk into a wooden trough.

Seven little pigs came from the corner, and one of them climbed into the trough. Mayflower pushed it back onto the ground with her snout. Randall laughed. "That's no way to treat one of your children!" Mayflower slurped greedily. Another of the pigs climbed into the trough and she pushed it aside. "Careful!" said Randall. "That's next year's bacon!" He knew that although she might appear to treat the piglets roughly herself, she was a good mother and would attack anyone or anything that bothered them.

After he had seen to the rest of his chores, Randall returned to the house. He could smell biscuits baking the moment he went inside. It was a wonderful aroma. His mother had baked biscuits every morning, but Aunt Earnestine usually gave the family store-bought bread.

Ida was at the stove, stirring a big pot of grits, and the twins stood off to the side, looking up at her. Randall heard her say, "Of course, that was before I did my bareback riding."

Clay said, "I thought you rode horseback."

"I did."

"But just now you said *bare*back."

Randall supposed Ida would learn that Clay always insisted on keeping to the exact truth. Sometimes the truth to Clay was more *exact* than to anyone else. "She doesn't mean she rode bears," he said. "She means the horse she rode was bareback, that it didn't have a saddle or anything on it."

Clay looked at him. "It had her on it, didn't it?"

Before Randall could answer, Ida said, "Of course I was talking about bears!" Then she lowered her voice as if she were telling a secret. "But to tell you the truth, I never did ride bears bareback. Nor buffaloes, either. For them I had a little red saddle with white fringe around it, and I'd go skipping out in a costume that made me look like a valentine and hop onto their backs."

"Then what'd happen?" asked Dewey.

Ida stirred the grits again and turned away from the stove. "Why, I'd go riding away, yelling 'Yippee!' as loud as I could. Like this." At that, she jumped into the air, clicked her heels together and yelled "Yippee!" so loud that dishes rattled in the cupboard. Then she skipped a few steps, jumped into the air, and yelled "Yippee!" again. "Come on, try it!" she told the twins, and the three of them circled the kitchen, skipping, jumping, and yelling.

Aunt Earnestine burst into the room. "What on earth is going on?" she asked.

"Just calling everybody to breakfast!" said Ida Early, panting a little. "No point in cooking a meal if nobody's gonna get up and eat it."

"It's still early," said Aunt Earnestine disgustedly, just as Mr. Sutton came into the room. "And today's Sunday."

"Why, so it is!" said Ida. "Where do you keep the whiskey?"

"This is not a drinking household," said Aunt Earnestine severely.

"Of course not!" said Ida. "Whiskey's not for drinking, it's for flavoring. A spoonful in the dessert would be just right."

"Dessert for breakfast? Oh, boy!" said Dewey, smiling as he sat down to his place at the table.

"A little boiled custard I whipped up for dinner," said Ida, but when Dewey's smile disappeared she added, "Why not for breakfast? That's a good idea, Dewey. It shows you're thinking! But you must eat your eggs first."

By the time Ellen came to the table, the blessing had been asked and everyone else was eating. Mr. Sutton seemed especially pleased. "Sawmill gravy!" he said happily when Ida served the bowl of thickened gravy that she had made from bacon drippings, milk, and flour. "When have we had sawmill gravy?"

"Not since Mamma died," said Clay. There was a brief silence, and Randall thought about his mother. It was still difficult to believe that she was gone. Often he imagined she was no farther away than the next room. He could hear her saying on the morning she was taken to the hospital, "I'll be back before the dogwoods bloom." Two weeks later, on the day of her funeral, a dogwood tree in the cemetery had been so filled with blossoms that it had looked like a white cloud.

"Now!" said Ida Early. "Who's for some boiled custard?"

"Everybody!" said Randall, getting up to help serve it.

"If you think a drop of whiskey would help," said Mr. Sutton, "there's a fruit jar of it in the pantry, just back of the syrup bucket."

Ida flavored the custard with a very small amount of whiskey, and when she had ladled out the custard she grated nutmeg on top. Everyone liked it. Even Aunt Earnestine was impressed. "I can never get it so smooth," she said. "This is delicious."

"Why, thank you, ma'am," said Ida. "I learned to make it when I was cooking for a family over in Gatlinburg."

Her tone of voice was different when she said it, and Randall looked at her. He suspected she was telling the truth, which he had decided did not come natural to her. He certainly didn't believe those stories she told. Maybe Aunt Earnestine's compliment had thrown her off guard. A compliment from Aunt Earnestine would throw anybody off guard.

Clay and Dewey looked up at Ida as if they were disappointed to hear that she had done anything so ordinary as cook for a family in Gatlinburg. Ida looked down at them and smiled. "No," she said, "now I remember where I learned to make boiled custard. It was when I was the head-knocker cook on a big ship."

"Was it a pirate ship?" asked Dewey.

"Of course it was!" said Ida. "I wouldn't fool around with any other kind."

Bath Time!

"It's only a stopgap measure," said Mr. Sutton.

"Well, I don't care," said Aunt Earnestine. "Isn't there anyone else?"

Randall, at the table by the lamp, pretended to be interested only in the book he was reading. Except for the three of them, everyone else had gone to bed. His father and his aunt were having a discussion about Ida Early.

Mr. Sutton said, "Eventually I'll find a permanent housekeeper, but in the meantime we'll just have to get by with this woman. At least, it gives you a chance to go back to Atlanta."

Aunt Earnestine sighed. "I certainly need to do that. I've neglected my own house and business affairs much too long."

"I know you have, Earnestine," said Mr. Sutton, "and I really appreciate all you've done. You've saved our lives."

"Maybe Myrtle would come manage things for you till you can find someone else," said Aunt Earnestine. Myrtle was their sister who lived in Knoxville.

"No, she needs to look after Ross and Kathy Alice." Ross was her husband and Kathy Alice their eight-year-old daughter.

"Ross could look after himself for a while, and she could bring Kathy Alice with her."

"Deliver me!" said Mr. Sutton, and Randall tried not to smile. Aunt Myrtle was as bossy as Aunt Earnestine, and Kathy Alice was a spoiled brat. Randall dreaded even a visit with Kathy Alice; he couldn't imagine having to live in the same house with her. He was glad that his father squelched the idea.

Two days later Aunt Earnestine went back to Atlanta, and Ida Early moved into her room and was put in charge of the Sutton household. Naturally, Ida had her own ways of going about the job. Meals were good, and Randall noticed she never scolded them, the way Aunt Earnestine had, about their table manners or for using too much catsup or spilling anything.

There was seldom a dessert except on Sundays. On other days at the end of a meal Randall and the twins loved to stick their finger in a biscuit, make a hollow place, and then fill it with syrup. Somehow it tasted better than putting a piece of bread on a plate, pouring syrup over it, and eating it with a fork—Aunt Earnestine's way. Ida Early not only let them jab holes in biscuits for the syrup—she did the same thing herself.

Also, she kept the house clean, but she wasn't a fanatic about it. "A little dust and a spider web or two help hold a house together," she would say, putting down the broom to play a game with the four of them. On days that she took cleaning more seriously, when she came to the twins she would pretend they were pieces of furniture and run the feather duster over them.

One day Dewey ran ahead of her. "Do it again," he said.

"Nope," said Ida. "Not this time." She threw the duster across the room. It landed, handle down, in the umbrella stand. "Good shot!" she said. She went over to the cookstove then and began pouring water from the kettles into a big washtub on the floor. "Bath time!" she said.

"Aw, do we have to take a bath?" asked Dewey. It had always been difficult to persuade Clay or Dewey that they needed to bathe. Randall, at the woodbox sharpening his pocketknife, wondered if Ida would succeed where almost everyone else had failed.

Clay said emphatically, "We're clean. We don't need a bath."

"Not *your* bath time," said Ida. *"My* bath time." At that, the twins hurried over and stood beside the tub as if they had been invited to come watch.

Ida took a washcloth and ran it over her face. "There," she said, reaching for the towel.

After she had hung up the towel, she said, "Anybody else?" Instead of waiting for an answer, she reached down, grabbed Clay under one arm and Dewey under the other and dropped them into the tub, clothes and all. Randall had never seen such kicking or heard such shrieks. "Hey!" he yelled. "You're splashing water over here!"

"It'll dry!" yelled Ida, and she and the twins whooped and yelled at each other. All the while she was lathering them with soap.

Ellen came in from the yard. "What's going on in here?" she asked. "I could hear the noise all the way out to the swing."

"You sound like Aunt Earnestine!" said Randall, imitating her: *"What's going on in here?"*

Ellen poked out her tongue at him, but when she saw Ida and the twins she laughed. "I never heard of anybody taking a bath without undressing first."

"Their clothes needed washing too," explained Ida. She and the twins continued to laugh and splash until she helped them out of their clothes, rinsed them off and dried them. "Now scoot in yonder and find the duds I put on the bed for you. See who can get dressed and buttoned up the quickest!"

"The whole room's wet," said Ellen.

"It's gonna get wetter," said Ida, dumping the tub of water onto the floor. "Shouldn't waste soapy water!" Randall lifted his feet when the water flowed near him, and Ellen raced to the back porch just ahead of a small wave. Ida took a corn-shuck mop and began scrubbing the floor.

By the time Mr. Sutton arrived home from work, the house was clean and so were the twins. And there was fried chicken for supper.

Close Call

Randall's friend, J. C., lived a mile down the road, but neither he nor Randall used the road when they visited each other. They had a well-worn path through the woods. It wasn't a shortcut; the road was more direct, but the woods were more interesting. There were hazards—snakes, wildcats, and bears, among them, but the boys knew that these creatures were unlikely to bother anyone unless they were disturbed first.

One afternoon J. C. knocked at the back door.

He held his brother, two-year-old Archie, in his arms. "Mamma's gone to town and left Archie for me to look after," he said, pausing to catch his breath, "and we decided to come up here and see what's going on."

"Nothing's going on," said Ellen, standing in the doorway. "Nothing ever happens up here, but come in. We've been missing you." Aunt Earnestine had scolded J. C. so severely about tracking a bit of mud into the house one afternoon that he had not been back for a while.

Randall, involved in a game of tiddlywinks with the twins, lifted a hand in greeting.

Ida Early, lying on her back on a rag rug just inside the door, was reading the *Progressive Farmer*, a magazine. Ellen stepped over her as if she were a log and went back to a jigsaw puzzle that was spread out on the table.

J. C. stood in the doorway. He looked down at Ida and then at Randall.

"That's Ida Early," said Randall.

"Who?"

"Ida Early. She's helping us."

"Helping you *what*?" asked J. C.

"Helping them with their aim," said Ida, rolling up the magazine. "Ladies and gentlemen, from the prone position!" She said it as if she were making

44

an announcement. Then, still lying on her back, she threw the *Progressive Farmer* across the room. It landed on the small stand beside Mr. Sutton's big chair.

"Just where it belongs!" said Ida, springing to her feet so quickly that little Archie grabbed J. C. around the neck and clung to him. "Happy to meet you!" said Ida, holding out her hand.

"Likewise, I reckon," said J. C., shifting Archie to his other arm and shaking hands with Ida.

When a new tiddlywinks game got under way, everyone played except Archie. He climbed over the players till he upset the board—which upset the players. "That's all right," said Ida, "you didn't mean to do it." Soon he was snuggled in her lap.

At the end of the game Ida said, "Better not start another one. Time to do the chores or dark'll catch us."

"We don't have any chores," said Clay.

"No, but you'd better get out in the fresh air for a while, anyway."

Randall took the milking bucket from the shelf over the icebox. "I hate milking!" he said. "You're lucky, J. C., to have older brothers. Otherwise you'd get stuck with the job."

Ida, folding up the tiddlywinks board, said,

"I never did mind milking."

Clay asked, "Are you gonna do the milking for Randall?"

"That's not what I had in mind," said Ida. "I just thought it might comfort him to know that not everybody hates the task the way he does."

"It'd be more comfort if you took over the job for me," said Randall.

J. C. looked at Ida and grinned. "I'll bet you don't even know how to milk!"

Ida, affecting a hurt tone, said, "Why, J. C., you're our neighbor and my new friend! How could you doubt me? Why, I don't suppose any of you would ever guess that—"

"I would," said Dewey. "I'd guess it, Ida Early."

"Guess what?"

"That you were once-upon-a-time champion milker of the whole big world."

"How ever did you know?" asked Ida, astonished.

"I just guessed it," explained Dewey.

"To tell you the truth," said Ida, "I was about to say that I don't even know what a cow looks like!" She pulled a bag of tobacco from the bib pocket of her overalls and began to roll a cigarette. As usual, she used only one hand. Randall glanced at J. C., who watched in disbelief.

Randall decided there was something to be said

for outright liars. At least, *he* knew never to believe anything they said. But Ida puzzled him. He still couldn't tell for certain when she might be telling the truth and when she was making up some whopper of a lie. There was no doubt that she could throw anything with deadly accuracy. But tame lions? Or ride mustangs? Maybe she made those stories up for the enjoyment of the twins.

He did not have to wait long to know which was the truth.

Ida reached over and took the milking bucket from him. "I'll do the milking for you if you'll start a fire in the stove. Fair enough?"

"Fair enough!" said Randall.

"Don't build a big fire," said Ida as she started out. "Everything's cooked but the biscuits." Often she prepared food in the middle of the day for lunch and supper. But all the Suttons were partial to hot biscuits, and Ida baked fresh ones every meal.

Ellen returned to her jigsaw puzzle, and the twins and Archie went outside. Randall started a fire in the cookstove, and then he took the bucket of table scraps from back of the stove, poured leftover buttermilk from the churn into it, and he and J. C. went outside to feed Mayflower.

Clay, Dewey, and Archie were at the edge of the

.woodpile, building a house from pieces of kindling and stovewood. One of the twins' pet chickens, a red rooster, stood nearby, watching as if the house were for him. Farther along, almost to the barn, one of Mayflower's pigs was playing at the edge of the path. Randall said to it, "You ain't supposed to be out!"

"Want me to help put it back in the pen?" asked J. C.

"Let's feed its mammy first," said Randall. "Then we'll see about it."

Mayflower was snoozing in the late afternoon sun, stretched out on her side. "Sooey!" yelled Randall, and she sprang to her feet and was at the trough before he had finished emptying the bucket into it. He was always surprised at how fast she could move when the notion struck her. She slurped noisily, stopping occasionally to snarl.

"Shut up and eat!" said Randall. "Nobody's gonna bother your young 'uns." The little pigs, all except the one in the path, played in a mudhole near the end of the trough.

"Here's where that 'un got out," said J. C., shaking a board that had come loose from a post.

"Yeah, that's it," agreed Randall. "Let's go find the hammer and some nails."

The hammer was not in the toolshed, and they went into the house to look for it. When it had been located, propped against the cupboard, they went back outside. The twins had moved from the woodpile to the swing by then, but Archie was not with them. He had wandered out toward the barn and was leaning over the little pig. The pig was rooting in the soft dirt at the edge of the path, and Randall could tell that Archie was about to pounce on it. "Don't!" he shouted, but it was too late. Archie grabbed at the pig. It almost got away, but he held to one of its back feet. The pig squealed so loudly that it could have been heard across the mountain.

In the pigsty Mayflower, snarling ferociously, rammed the fence in an attempt to get out, and the loose board fell to the ground. She shot through the gap and ran toward Archie, who still held onto the pig. "Let it go!" screamed Randall as he and J. C. ran toward him. There was no way they could head off the angry sow; they were too far away. Suddenly Ida Early dashed from the barn. She reached Archie just as Mayflower was almost to him. Kicking at the sow with one foot, Ida grabbed Archie and made him let go of the pig. She kicked Mayflower away again with walloping force.

When the little pig was set free, it stopped its squealing, and Mayflower's snarl became an angry grunt.

Ida transferred Archie, who did not realize how narrowly he'd escaped real injury, to J. C.'s arms. Then she picked up a stick and scratched Mayflower's side with it. This had a soothing effect on the sow, and Ida carried on a conversation with her. "I know you were only protecting your own young 'un. But you could've killed Archie."

Randall said, "She would have if you hadn't stopped her." Mayflower snarled as if she still might consider it, and J. C. backed away, holding Archie tightly.

"No more of that!" said Ida, and she tapped Mayflower on the snout with the stick. The sow, although she snarled again, did not make a move toward anyone. Ida took the stick then and gently drove Mayflower and the piglet back into the pen.

Maybe she *had* tamed lions.

Country Club

"Let's play something," said Dewey. He was sitting on the laundry bench, leaning against one of the big galvanized tubs, while Randall, across the path at the woodpile, stacked kindling. "You said when you finished chopping, you'd play."

Randall straightened up. His shoulder muscles hurt from swinging the ax, and he stretched his arms out to the side. "All right," he said, "what'll we play?"

"Whatever you want to," said Dewey.

Randall stretched again. "We could play hiding," he said. "Run in the house and see if Ellen and Clay'll come out."

"They won't. I already asked them."

"I know what," said Randall. "I've thought of a new game. It's called Country Club."

"Like the one Aunt Earnestine told us about?" Their aunt had mentioned once that she lived near a country club in Atlanta, and the twins had not been able to understand how anything called a *country* club could be in the city.

"Yeah," said Randall, "only ours'll be in the loft of the barn. To join"—he thought for a minute— "you have to knock twice on the barn door and give the password good and loud. If you get it right, you can climb up the ladder to the loft and we'll have a club meeting, okay?"

"What's the password?"

"Let me think," said Randall. "How about 'burlap bag'? Can you remember it?"

"You mean a feed sack?"

"Yeah, it's the same thing. Give me a head start, and then you come ahead."

Randall hurried into the big hall of the barn. There were two feed rooms and a stall on one side and three stalls on the other. To get to the loft it was necessary to go through the first feed room and up a ladder that was nailed to the wall. Randall's father had told him that in earlier days the big loft was often filled with hay. Wagon loads of it could be driven up to the front of the barn; the hay was then pitched into the loft through a big window above the double doors. The Suttons did not need a barn of that size, but the extra room was a good place to play. Randall grabbed a burlap bag from the first feed room and climbed the ladder to the loft. He leaned out the window just as Dewey arrived at the door underneath.

Dewey knocked twice and called out, "Burlap bag!"

Randall dropped the bag onto Dewey, and it covered him like a net. Dewey began sputtering and flailing at the bag. It looked funny. By the time he was free of it, Randall had climbed to the ground, still smiling.

"What was that for?" asked Dewey, with a hurt look on his face.

"It's the new game."

"I don't like it," said Dewey.

"Aw, it didn't hurt you," Randall said, putting his hand on Dewey's shoulder. "It was a joke—can't you take a joke?"

"No," said Dewey, but a moment later, while Randall shucked corn for Mayflower, he suggested they play the joke on Clay.

"All right," said Randall, "but let's change the

password. That bag dropping over you wasn't much fun, was it?" He put his arm around Dewey. "I meant to scare you a little, not a lot."

"Let's scare Clay a lot," said Dewey.

Randall laughed. "No, let's think of something else." Looking at the pile of shucks beside him, he said, "I'll take some of these to the loft, and you and I'll drop them on Clay's head Go invite him to join, and tell him the password is 'corn shucks.' "

In a little while Dewey came running back. "He's coming! He's coming!" he said excitedly, and he and Randall hurried to the loft. They forgot the shucks, and Randall barely had time to fetch them before Clay was there.

Clay called, "Hey, where are you?"

Randall lowered his voice and tried to make it sound scary. "Who's there?"

"It's me," said Clay. "Where are you?"

"What do you want?" asked Randall in his low voice.

"I wanna play Country Club."

"But do you know the password?"

"It's corn shucks," yelled Clay. "Now where—"

At that the corn shucks were dropped onto him, and Randall and Dewey hurried to the ground. Dewey laughed as if there had never been anything funnier. "Did it scare you?" he asked.

"No," said Clay, disgustedly brushing himself off.

"What'd you think," asked Randall, "when you said, 'Corn shucks,' and all of a sudden shucks started falling on you?"

"I thought it was stupid."

"It was a joke," said Dewey, the way Randall had said it to him. "Can't you take a joke?"

"Jokes are funny," said Clay, scowling. "That wasn't funny."

"It was so," insisted Dewey, and he laughed more.

Randall smiled at Clay, who still looked furious. "It wasn't so funny to Dewey either when the joke was on him." This did not cheer up Clay; he walked away angrily. But halfway to the house, he turned and came back. "Let's ask Ellen to join the country club," he said.

For Ellen, the password was changed to "an armload of hay," and when it was dropped onto her head, she complained, "That's the silliest game I ever heard of." But when J. C. came along soon afterward it was she who suggested that he might like to play their new game. "It's called Country Club," she said, "and we meet in the barn loft." The twins giggled. "Let's see," said Ellen. "What should the password be?"

"Oh," said Randall, "how about 'corn shucks, hay, and a burlap bag'?"

"That should do," said Ellen. She explained the rules to J. C. while everyone else hurried to the club room.

When J. C. was showered with the "password," he jumped as if he'd been shot. But he soon got over the scare. "Too bad there's nobody else to play it on," he said as he climbed up the ladder. He and the Suttons sat for a while in the club room. No one would admit to having been frightened or even terribly surprised when the password had turned out to be something dropped from the loft window. Then the talk turned to school and how it would be starting in a few weeks. Randall didn't mind it. He and J. C. were going into the sixth grade, and Mrs. Long, the teacher, was all right. "She's not mean like Mrs. Putney," said J. C.

"Now stop teasing Dewey and Clay!" said Ellen. The twins would be six in the fall and were to start school. Mrs. Putney was the first-grade teacher. "Mrs. Putney's nice."

"Nice if you like to get a switching every time you turn around!" said J. C.

"She doesn't use the switch unless you deserve it," insisted Ellen. "And Clay and Dewey are going to behave so well they'll get along fine."

"We're not going to school," said Clay.

"Of course you are!" said Ellen. "There's no way to get out of going to school."

"We'll stay home with Ida Early," said Dewey.

"Say!" said J. C. "Why don't we ask Ida Early to join the country club?"

Everyone laughed and began trying to think of a good password. Finally they agreed that it should be: An armload of hay, a burlap bag, two green apples, corn shucks, and a dipperful of water.

Randall ran to the well to draw a bucket of water, and when he had returned with a dipperful of it, the twins were back with a green apple each. Ellen had gathered some hay and corn shucks together.

J. C., who was to have the burlap bag, had gone to the house to ask Ida if she would care to join. Soon he scurried into the loft. "She's coming!" he said.

Clay and Dewey peeked out the window. Randall told them to stay hidden or she'd see them. "I'll keep watch," he said, and everyone else ducked out of sight. "She's starting along the path," he said a moment later. "No, wait a minute! She's turned back toward the house."

Everyone peeked out again. They watched as Ida pulled weeds from around a wildflower growing at the edge of the path. Randall asked J. C., "Are you sure she said she'd come out here?"

"I'm sure."

Ellen asked, "Reckon she can remember that long password?"

J. C. laughed. "I asked her if she could, and she said she has such a good memory that she can recall things that never even happened."

Just then Ida left off the weed pulling and headed toward the barn. Everyone ducked out of sight, but after a few moments Randall risked peeking out once more. Ida had arrived at the woodpile. She appeared to be looking at the big stack of kindling that he had chopped. Then she looked toward the barn, and Randall decided he had better stay out of sight.

"Where was she?" whispered Dewey.

"She was almost to the laundry bench," said Randall. "She should be here soon." He did not look out again, and finally there was a loud knock on the barn door.

"Who's there?" called Ellen so sweetly that the twins and J. C. snickered.

"Somebody to join up with the country club."

"What's the password?"

"Well, now," said Ida, "I've forgot it already." Everyone in the loft sighed. "But if you wouldn't mind waiting a bit, it might come back to me."

"Tell her we'll wait," whispered Randall.

"The club is willing to wait," called Ellen. "Think hard!"

Ida said cheerily, "I'll try! I remember that it was an armload of something. Dirty clothes? An armload of dirty clothes? No, that's not it. But just wait, I'll remember. Yeah, I think it's come back to me now. How does this sound to you: An armload of hay, some corn shucks, a feed sack or a burlap bag, whichever you care to call it, two green apples, and a dipperful of cold well water."

The twins dropped the apples, Ellen tossed the hay and corn shucks, J. C. hurled the burlap bag and Randall dribbled the well water. Then they scrambled to see out. Beneath them, all they could see was the bottom of a washtub that Ida held upside down over her head. At her feet were the hay and the corn shucks. The apples had rolled away. Ida laughed as she put the tub on the ground.

The children were disappointed. "We wanted to scare you!" said Clay.

J. C. asked, "How'd you guess it, Ida? How'd you know what might happen?"

Ida said, "What do you think I've been doing if I haven't been standing at the kitchen window watching all the fun that was going on out here? I guess I outfoxed everybody, didn't I?" She went into the barn and climbed up the ladder. "And I suppose that means I get to be president of the country club." She sat down cross-legged on the loft floor and said, "A club meeting will now come to order!" Then, after everyone was settled, the president told funny stories till milking time.

Randall and Ellen talked later about how Ida might have taken it if she'd been surprised, like everyone else, when "passwords" showered down from the barn loft. "She'd have laughed," said Ellen.

"Yeah, she probably would have," agreed Randall. "I doubt anything gets the best of her."

The twins were across the room, coloring yesterday's comic strips with crayons. Randall hadn't realized they were listening till Dewey said, "Nothing could *ever* get the best of Ida!"

The Early Aim
and the Carnival

The week before school was to start there was a
fair in Buckley. At lunch on Saturday Mr. Sutton
told his family, "I had hoped to take you, but we
have a rush order at the yard." He was talking
about the lumberyard, where he was foreman. "So
I must work."

They all groaned.

"But you can go without me," said Mr. Sutton,
"provided Ida'll watch over you."

"It would pleasure me," said Ida, and as soon as

everyone had finished eating, Ida and the children rode as far as the lumberyard with Mr. Sutton. They would walk across town to the fair.

Just as they crossed the main street, Ellen's friend Nancy Parker came out of the drugstore. The boys and Ida Early waited while Ellen chatted with her. Randall had never liked Nancy. She was always bragging about the advantages town children had over the ones who lived in the country. At the moment she was telling about a prom party that someone was planning. "We're to wear evening dresses," said Nancy, "and I'm not sure I'll know how to act."

Ida Early, standing off to the side, said, "Just act natural."

Nancy looked at her, and Ida struck a match on the seat of her overalls and lit a cigarette.

"Are you related to the Suttons?" asked Nancy in a tone that meant she certainly hoped not.

"Not a bit," said Ida. She blew a perfect smoke ring and added, "I'm their girlfriend."

Nancy suddenly remembered she'd forgotten something in the drugstore and hurried back inside.

Ida started away, holding Dewey by one hand and Clay by the other. Randall and Ellen lagged behind.

Randall laughed about Nancy rushing away in a

huff, but Ellen didn't think it was funny. "Ida's an embarrassment sometimes," she said disgustedly, but by the time they were at the fair she was in a better humor.

Ida said, "Randall, maybe you and Ellen would have fun going your own way for a while."

"What about us?" asked Clay.

"Well, I thought you and Dewey and I'd have a good time on some of the rides that might not interest anybody else. We'll get back together at nearer time to go home."

"Fine," said Randall.

"Here's part of the money that your pa gave us," said Ida, handing Ellen and Randall more than half of it. "Spend it however you like."

When they were separating, Ellen said, "Don't anybody fall off the merry-go-round!"

"We won't," promised Dewey, who had fallen off one of the horses at last year's fair.

"Don't fall off anything!" cautioned Randall.

"Me or Dewey?" asked Clay.

"Neither of you!" said Randall. "Stay close to Ida and behave!"

Randall and Ellen went first to the Ferris wheel, and while they were waiting in line Marcus Ragsdale came along. "Come ride with us," invited Randall, and Marcus was quick to accept. This, of course, pleased Ellen, and after the ride the three of them walked around the midway together. An hour later they were back where they had started. J. C. had joined them, and he and Randall stood watching the Loop-o'-Sky, a ride that was new to the fair this year. It was like a giant pendulum, and riders, fastened in a cage-like compartment, were swung back and forth until it eventually went over. Then it went over and over, faster and faster, and the compartment spun around at the same time. More people watched it than had the nerve to get on it.

J. C. said, "I dare you to ride it!"

"I'm trying to get up courage," said Randall. "I'll ride it if you will!"

"Not me!" said J. C., looking up at the compartment that was spinning around at the same time it looped over. "It makes me dizzy just to watch!"

Randall was saying that he believed he'd hold off till another year to take a ride on it when the Loop-o'-Sky came to a halt. An attendant unfastened the door and opened it, and out came Clay, Dewey, and Ida Early.

Randall laughed. "I thought you'd be over at the kiddie cars!"

"We like this best," said Dewey, glancing back at the Loop-o'-Sky. "This was our third time."

Later, when Randall and Ellen had rejoined Ida and the twins, Ida said, "Now that our money's gone, we'll be able to enjoy things even more. We won't be hindered by having to decide how to spend anything." She led the way through the midway again, stopping whenever there was anything interesting to watch. At one of the sideshows a barker was calling, "Get your tickets here! See the fattest woman in the world and the littlest man. Get your tickets here!"

At the next tent another barker called, "A free show every fifteen minutes! Step right up, the next free show is about to begin!" More than a dozen people had already stopped, and others drew near. "Step right up!" called the barker. "See the freaks!"

Clay whispered, "What're freaks?"

"Funny-looking things," answered Ellen.

"Only they're not really funny," explained Ida. "They're mostly things nature has played mean tricks on."

"Here comes one now," said Randall, and he lifted Dewey onto his shoulders so that he could see over the heads of the people in front. Ida lifted Clay.

A thin young man with matted, blond hair and a beard was led onto the platform. "A genuine wild man from the tribes of a far-off jungle," said the barker. "Savage one hundred per cent, he eats frogs, lizards, and live birds. Don't stand too near him, folks, he could be dangerous." The wild man did not look dangerous. There was a vacant expression in his eyes as if he did not know what was going on around him, and he stood shivering in the warm sunshine as if he were freezing to death.

"We shouldn't gape at other people's misfortunes," said Ida. "Let's go see something else." She led the way to the ball-throwing concession. There was a stand near the front of it, off to one side, filled with horse statues that were the prizes. They were all the same shape and size but different colors. The mane of each one had been sprinkled with gold or silver glitter. Clay and Dewey stopped to admire the horses while everyone else watched three men who were throwing baseballs at stuffed dolls.

The dolls were about the size of milk bottles and fitted snugly into a wooden rack. There were four rows of them. "Topple a doll! Topple a doll!" called the barker.

The biggest of the three men, called Noon by his companions, knocked over one of the dolls, but on his next try he missed. "That ball was off balance," he said, throwing another one. It hit a doll in the top row but did not knock it over. "Hey!" he yelled. "You've got some of 'em nailed down."

The barker walked over to the rack and lifted the doll out of it. He called to the crowd, "Hit 'em right and they'll fall every time! Step up, neighbors, and try your luck!"

The man, Noon, paid for more baseballs. He knocked over a few of the dolls with them, but whenever he missed he blamed the balls or the targets.

Ida opened the bib pocket of her overalls and began looking through it. Clay asked, "Did you lose your tobacco?"

"No," said Ida, still searching. "Ah, here it is!" She held up a dime. "I've been saving this for a special occasion. Maybe I'll throw baseballs with it."

"Will you win a prize?" asked Dewey, looking at the plaster-of-Paris horses.

"Maybe," said Ida, turning to the barker. "What must I do to win a horse for my friends here?"

"Throw five times, knock over three dolls," he said. "There's nothing to it."

Ida paid him, took the baseballs, and in rapid-fire order she knocked over a doll with each one. "Nothing to it!" she told the barker, who looked as if he couldn't believe what he'd seen. Two young couples standing nearby cheered. "Why, thank you," said Ida, bowing. She explained to them that it was all in the wrist movement, while Dewey and Clay tried to decide which horse they wanted.

One of the men with Noon said, "Hey, woman, Noon challenges you to a contest!"

"Aw, no, I don't!" said Noon.

"Thank you," said Ida, "but I wasn't planning to do any more throwing."

"Come on," insisted the man, "be a sport!" Randall didn't know if he was saying it to Noon or Ida.

A small crowd had gathered by then, and the barker told Ida, "I'll stake you. What's the bet to be?"

"We won't gamble on the outcome," she said. "But if you'd like us to have a friendly contest I'll be pleased to test my aim with, say, ten throws."

Noon did not look happy about it, but his friends were saying things like, "Are you afraid a woman can beat you?" and, "All you've got to lose is your self-respect!" They laughed as if they'd made the funniest jokes anybody had ever heard.

Noon threw the first ball and knocked over a doll. Ida said, "I can't beat that!" and wound up for her first try. She threw the ball, and it barely missed a doll. Splinters flew from the edge of the rack.

Noon threw again and knocked over another doll, and so did Ida. Their next three shots were hits, also, and toppled a doll each time.

The contest continued. Noon missed his sixth

shot, knocked over a doll on the seventh, and then missed three times in a row. Ida knocked over a doll with every throw except the first one. At the end Noon turned to her and said, "You oughta join up with the carnival!" Everybody who had gathered around laughed.

"Why, thank you," said Ida, smiling at him. "I'm glad you think I'm *that* good."

"I don't," said Noon. "I think you belong in a freak show!" He turned and started away, laughing loudly. "Anybody as funny-looking as you are belongs in a freak show!" he called back. His two pals followed him.

The crowd seemed not to know what to do. Some of them snickered, and a few looked embarrassed. Ida's smile disappeared. Randall felt bad for her; he knew that being laughed at could be painful. He wished the crowd would break up instead of standing around as if there'd be another show.

Ida looked at the barker. "Thank you," she said, and he only nodded.

"We'd better go," said Randall.

"Yes," agreed Ida, and she led the children away. Dewey carried the blue horse with the silver mane that he and Clay had chosen.

On the edge of the road, heading home, Ida walked first, Dewey holding to one of her hands.

Randall was next, then Ellen, and Clay was last. Nobody said anything for a long time; then Clay hurried to the front of the line. Taking Ida by her other hand, he said, "I don't think you're funny-looking."

"Don't you, really?" asked Ida. Randall hoped that Clay would not suddenly change his mind.

"No," said Clay earnestly. "I think you're prettier than anybody in the whole big world."

Ida laughed. "Why, thank you," she said. "I think so, too!" Then everyone laughed and walked along with a springier step.

Sunday Visitors

Aunt Myrtle, Uncle Ross, and Kathy Alice came to spend the first Sunday in September. Aunt Myrtle was feared by the children only slightly less than Aunt Earnestine. In Randall's opinion, Aunt Myrtle was more of a gunboat than a battleship. Her presence was not always overpowering, but it was usually best to get out of her way. She was a small woman and Uncle Ross was a big hulk of a man. Their daughter, Kathy Alice, was average size for an eight-year-old. Mr. Sutton once described

Kathy Alice as being "loud for her age."

When Aunt Myrtle's family arrived, the Suttons were in the yard. It was a warm day, and Mr. Sutton had taken off his coat and thrown it over one arm. He and his children had just arrived home from church.

"My, it's good to see all of you," said Aunt Myrtle. "From Earnestine's report, I didn't know how I'd find you."

Uncle Ross said, "I told you they'd be all right."

"You look well," said Aunt Myrtle.

"Of course we do," said Mr. Sutton. "We have on our Sunday finery."

"I mean you look healthy," said Aunt Myrtle, glancing around at each one. "Some of your Sunday finery could do with pressing."

Mr. Sutton pulled at his collar. "The shirt was a little fresher early this morning, but so was I."

"Ellen, your dress looks nice," said Aunt Myrtle.

"It's pressed!" said Mr. Sutton, laughing as he patted Ellen on the back. "And she made it herself."

"Did you really?"

"Yes, ma'am. In home economics last spring."

Aunt Myrtle looked at Randall and the twins. "What happened to *their* clothes?"

"They didn't take home economics," said Mr. Sutton.

Aunt Myrtle did not smile. "Their shirts don't look as if they've seen the flat side of an iron. Ever!"

"Myrtle!" said Randall's father. "Can't you wait till we're sitting down to start pointing out our errors?"

"But Earnestine and I have been so worried about all of you."

"All of us are fine. Now come onto the porch where it's cooler, and let's not argue." He winked at Randall, who knew there'd be arguments all day.

The twins took Kathy Alice to play in the backyard, and Ellen went inside to help Ida Early with the cooking. Randall and his father sat with Aunt Myrtle and Uncle Ross on the porch till they were called to dinner. As they started inside, Aunt Myrtle said, "Now Kathy Alice and I could come and look after your family for a while. Ross has agreed that we can."

"How often do I have to tell you that we're doing all right?"

"But you desperately need someone to keep house for you whether you realize it or not!"

"We have someone," said Mr. Sutton. "She may not do everything the way you or Earnestine would, but that's okay." He opened the door for them to go inside. "Come in and meet her."

Ida wore overalls on Sundays, the same as any other day, but with two added touches: Clipped to the left strap, just above the bib, was an artificial flower. It was big enough to have been a sunflower, but it was shaped more like a rose, and its faded color was purple. Clay and Dewey had found it down by the road a month ago. Someone told them that it had once decorated the top of a very big box of candy. They had made a present of it to Ida, who insisted that it was too pretty to wear every day but that she would certainly wear it on Sundays—if not all day, at Sunday dinner in any event. So far she had kept her promise.

The twins had been so pleased the first time she'd worn it that they had looked all the following week for another flower. They wanted Ida to have one to fasten to the right strap of her overalls. No more fake flowers appeared on the roadside, so they enlisted Ida's help in making one. The finished object looked more like a bedraggled feather duster than a flower, perhaps because it was made from chicken feathers they'd picked up in the yard. Mr. Sutton had called it "a Rhode Island Red" rose because that was the name of the breed of chickens. There were a few White Leghorns in the flock, and they were represented in Ida's second corsage too. Mr. Sutton had teased the twins. "You'd better not let Ida wear it outside," he had said. "A rooster might chase her across the yard!" Somehow the flowery and feathery touches made Sunday dinners, along with Ida's cooking, festive events.

When Aunt Myrtle went into the room, Ida was turned to the stove, taking a sweet-potato-and-raisin pie from the oven. When she turned around, Randall had to admit that she did look more like a feather-breasted giant than a person, and he believed for a moment that Aunt Myrtle was going to faint. She left off her conversation in mid-sentence, and when Mr. Sutton introduced her, saying, "This is Ida Early," all Aunt Myrtle said was, "Oh." Kathy Alice and the twins burst into the room at that moment, and there was confusion as everyone found a place at the table.

During the meal Uncle Ross, for a change, talked more than Aunt Myrtle. He kept saying how good the food was and that if it wasn't so far from Knoxville they'd come every Sunday for dinner. Even Aunt Myrtle could not find anything to criticize about the meal. Most of the conversation was about school, which was to start soon. The twins still insisted that they were not going; they would stay home with Ida Early.

When dinner was over, Ellen excused herself to go back to church. Her Sunday School class was to practice a program for the night service. The rest of the family went out to sit on the front porch.

Clay and Dewey played in the soft dirt at the edge of the steps where there had once been a sandbox. They tried to build castles with the soil, but it did not hold together well enough for anything grand. Their structures looked more like small igloos than anything else. Dewey molded an unusually big one over his foot; it did not cave in, the way most of them did, when he pulled his foot from it.

Ida came out of the house and sat down on the top step. "That's a jim-dandy frog house," she told Dewey. "Build another one!"

Aunt Myrtle asked, "Are the dishes washed already?" Of course, they weren't; the meal was just over. Randall knew it was Aunt Myrtle's way of telling Ida what she should be doing.

"Washed as they'll get for a while," said Ida, rolling a cigarette. "Care for a smoke?" She held out the bag of tobacco to Aunt Myrtle.

"Certainly not!" said Aunt Myrtle primly. There was a frosty silence.

Ida lit the cigarette and said, "I think I'll take me a walk."

"We want to go," said Clay and Dewey at the same time. They hopped up and started after her.

"You'd better stay here with Kathy Alice," said Ida. "She's your company."

"She can come with us," said Clay.

"I don't want to," said Kathy Alice.

Mr. Sutton called the twins back. "You can go to walk another time," he said firmly. "Let's visit with our kinfolks now, all right?"

Clay and Dewey did not agree that it was all right, but they did return to their frog houses. Kathy Alice had stepped on the good one that Dewey had built. He began to rebuild it.

Aunt Myrtle began to rail against Ida Early. Randall had known it was coming. He suspected that Ida had known it too; probably that was why she'd gone for a walk. "She's very strange," said Aunt Myrtle, "and you're crazy to put her in charge of your household."

"The house is kept well enough to suit us," said Mr. Sutton, "and my family's well fed."

"You can say that again!" said Uncle Ross, patting his stomach. "If it wasn't so far from Knoxville, we'd come every Sunday!" It was the third time he'd said it.

"What's more," said Mr. Sutton, "the children are happy for the first time in months. So if you and Earnestine could just—"

He was interrupted by Kathy Alice saying loudly, as if she hoped Ida might still be within earshot, "Ida Early's tacky-looking."

Dewey stood up. Glaring at Kathy Alice, he

said, "She *is not* tacky-looking."

"She is so," said Kathy Alice, "and she acts goofy."

Clay said, "She does not!"

"Now, now," said Mr. Sutton, "let's calm down. And I think it might be a good idea, Clay, if you and Dewey showed Kathy Alice the new swing."

"She's seen it," said Clay.

Mr. Sutton laughed, "Well, how about playing somewhere else, anyway?"

"We'll go swing," said Clay, as if the idea were his. He led the way toward the backyard.

"I don't want to swing," said Kathy Alice, but she trailed after the twins when she saw that they were going, whether she did or not.

Aunt Myrtle continued to point out the faults of Ida Early. Randall went inside and read for a while, and when he returned to the porch she was still insisting that Mr. Sutton find someone else. If not, she said, she would bring Kathy Alice and come for a while, welcome or not.

"Aw, Myrtle," said Mr. Sutton, "you know you're welcome any time."

Before he could say anything else, Kathy Alice ran onto the porch, stood between Aunt Myrtle and Mr. Sutton, and began counting loudly. Randall knew that if one of the twins had done such a thing, he'd have been given a swat on the seat and told to go somewhere else. But the grown-ups stopped talking till Kathy Alice had reached a hundred.

Mr. Sutton said, "Clay and Dewey should have had plenty of time to hide by now."

"We're not playing hiding," said Kathy Alice. "We're playing Country Club. And I'm gonna join."

"I've heard about Country Club," said Mr. Sutton pleasantly. "What's the password?"

"I'm not gonna tell you!"

"Now, dear heart," said Aunt Myrtle, "you must talk sweeter than that."

"I'm not gonna tell you either," said Kathy Alice, starting away. A moment later she poked her head around the corner of the house and said in an even more smart-alecky tone than usual, "I'm going out to the barn to join the country club, and for the benefit of people who think they have to know everything, the password is 'a bucket of mud.' " She dashed away.

"Oh, my goodness!" said Randall, springing to his feet. "I'd better catch her."

Aunt Myrtle grabbed him by the arm.

Mr. Sutton said, "Myrtle, you'd better let the boy go!"

"I'll do nothing of the sort," she said. "If Kathy Alice is enjoying a game with Clay and Dewey, the *older children* should leave them alone." She always said "older children" as if Randall and Ellen were an evil force out to get Kathy Alice.

"Have it your way," said Mr. Sutton. He pushed back in his chair and smiled at Randall. Randall smiled back.

Schoolyard

The twins refused to go to school. The first day of the term they made such a fuss that Ida let them stay home. "But you must go tomorrow," she said, "or we'll all be in trouble with your pa."

The next morning Clay and Dewey dressed for school, ate their breakfast, and hid in the loft of the barn till the bus went past. The next day they went to the bus stop but ran into the woods when the bus came along, and no one could catch them.

Finally they agreed to go to school if Ida would go with them. "Why?" she asked.

"To keep the teacher from whipping us," said Dewey.

"That teacher's not gonna whip you. You've been listening to too many tales Randall and J. C.'ve been telling you."

"We'll go if you'll go," said Clay.

"No," said Ida. "Why should I go?"

"Why should we go?" asked Clay.

" 'Cause I want you to," said Ida.

"We want you to go," insisted Clay.

"Oh, all right. Tomorrow I'll go with you, and I'll stay till recess."

"What's recess?" asked Dewey.

"That's when you play and have a good time. You won't mind doing that without me. But I'll go," she promised, "and I'll stay with you till then. Is that a bargain?"

Clay and Dewey looked at each other. Finally Clay nodded, and Dewey said, "I guess so."

"Okay, shake hands on it," said Ida. "No, not with each other. With me!" She clutched their hands together in hers and pumped them up and down. "Good!" she said, letting their hands go. "We've struck us a bargain, and there's no backing out. Do you understand?"

"We won't back out," promised Clay. "We'll go."

In the morning the twins did not try to get out of their agreement. Breakfast was earlier than usual so that they and Ida would have plenty of time to walk to school. Ida had doubted the driver would let her ride the bus with them, so the twins had agreed to walk with her. In the afternoon Ellen and Randall were to see that they returned home safely.

Grammar school, at one end of the long building, was separated from the high school by a big auditorium. Because high school students were allowed to use the gymnasium and the ball field, most of the schoolyard was considered a playground for the grammar school. At recess, children in the primary grades played in back of the building. The ones in the middle grades kept to the side of it, and the older boys and girls stayed in front.

Randall and his pals liked to gather at the end of the schoolyard. There was a high bank, overlooking the road, and they could watch any cars that went past. When there were no cars to watch, they chatted with—and sometimes teased—the girls who gathered at the big tree nearby. Ellen and her friends were usually near the tree, although this morning they had stopped somewhere else.

Joe Blakley said, "I hate school!"

"Just 'cause you didn't know the answer a while ago?" said Dan Rogers. Mrs. Long had caught Joe staring out the window instead of paying attention during math.

"Know the *answer*?" said Randall. "Joe didn't even know the *question*!" He and Dan laughed.

"That's okay, Joe," said Dan. "I knew the answer, but I hate school too."

"Yeah, me too!" said Randall, but he didn't mean it. It was easier to pretend that he disliked it than to try to explain his real feelings. In truth, he enjoyed school and was glad it had started back. After being home all summer, seldom seeing anyone outside the family, it was fun to be part of a bigger world. Lessons could be interesting—some he enjoyed more than others—but what he liked best was being with friends.

While he stood near the bank, he saw Ida coming around the corner of the building. Even though he'd known she was bringing the twins to school today, it seemed strange to see her here. She belonged in a different part of his life; it was as if she were in the wrong place now. Home, as he stood talking with Joe and Dan, seemed a long way off.

Randall half expected Clay and Dewey to come running after Ida—in spite of their promise to stay in school. He was relieved when she reached the end of the walkway and the twins had not yet appeared.

Joe, seeing Ida on the road, asked, "Who's that?"

"You mean, *what's* that?" asked Dan.

The question shocked Randall. Then he realized that Dan may never have seen a woman who was taller than most men. Too, it wasn't just her height that was noticeable to anyone who'd never seen Ida. It was a lot of things, including her overalls and clodhopper shoes and hair that looked like a frazzled hearth broom.

Ida looked up and saw the boys looking at her. "Howdy-do?" she called cheerily, waving at them with both hands.

Randall felt himself blush. He put up his hand feebly and waved back as Dan called, "Howdy-do to you! Are you a new student?"

"Could be!" answered Ida. "Or I could be a new teacher!"

A group of girls nearby giggled, and another group, including Daisy Coker and Fay Edison, called "the loudmouths" by their classmates in the sixth grade, walked over to the edge of the bank just as Dan asked, "What do you teach?"

"Didn't say I taught anything," said Ida. "I said I *could*."

"What *could* you teach?" he yelled back. More students, including Ellen and some of her friends, came out to the bank.

" 'Most anything!" answered Ida, stopping on the roadside and grinning up at the students who were looking down at her.

Daisy Coker yelled across to Dan, "She could teach home economics! Cain't you tell from those overalls that she knows all about styles?"

A lot of the boys and girls laughed. Ida did not look as if she thought it had been especially funny, but she kept grinning. "Why, thank you," she said. "I'm glad you approve of my outfit. But next time I'll try to wear something else if that would be better."

"Wear a clown suit!" shouted Fay Edison.

Ida laughed. "Now that's an idea! I've never thought of wearing a clown suit!"

Randall wished the bell would ring for recess to end. He could tell that Ida was more hurt than she let on.

"You don't need a clown suit," said Daisy.

"Yeah," added Fay, "you look funny enough as it is!" Their friends laughed loudly.

Ida's grin disappeared, and she looked at Randall but did not say anything to him. And she looked over at Ellen. Randall knew he should say something, tell their classmates that the joke had gone far enough and to leave Ida alone. But he couldn't speak.

Daisy called to Ida, "You act funny, too!"

Ida turned and started away. Daisy and Fay called after her, "Clown! Clown!" More boys and girls joined in. "Clown! Clown!" they shouted.

Dan reached down and picked up a pebble. He drew back his arm to throw it, and Ellen said, "Don't!"

"Aw, it won't hurt," said Dan. "It'll just scare 'er. I wanna see her jump!" He took aim again.

Randall grabbed Dan's arm and made him drop the stone, but he knew it was too late for Ida to know that anyone on the bank had acted at all like a friend.

After School

Randall went by the first grade, but Clay and Dewey were not there. "They left with the other children," said Mrs. Putney. "Weren't they to catch the bus?"

"No, ma'am. We're walking home today, and they were to wait here."

"You'd better run check the buses," said Mrs. Putney, and Randall hurried away. Just as he rounded a corner of the building, Clay and Dewey called to him from behind a clump of shrubbery. "Come help us!" called Dewey, and Randall ran to them. He was afraid they were in trouble.

"Reckon where they keep the shovel around here?" asked Clay. Pointing to a small hole in the ground, he said, "A chipmunk ran in this hole, and if we can find a shovel we'll dig it out."

"Aw, come on!" said Randall disgustedly. "And why didn't you wait in the room the way you were supposed to?"

"We just came outside a little way," said Dewey. "And then we saw the chipmunk."

"Well, that chipmunk's gone."

"No, it ran in this hole," insisted Clay.

"Yeah, but that hole probably goes to a tunnel that connects with another one till it comes out somewhere else."

"Where?"

"Anywhere," said Randall. Pointing toward a tree across the playground, he said, "Over there, maybe."

"Let's go look," said Dewey, but Randall grabbed each of the twins by a hand and led them away. "Ellen's waiting for us at the drugstore."

"The drugstore!" said Clay. "Oh, boy! Can we buy ice cream?"

"Maybe," said Randall, "if there's any money

left." He was thinking about the Monopoly set. They'd heard that the drugstore had a new shipment of games.

At the store Mrs. Dawson, the druggist's wife, said, "We're sold out of Monopoly." Leading them to a counter, she said, "But look around—you may see something you like better." She held up a small box. "Here are some Rook cards. Have you ever played Rook?"

"No, ma'am," said Randall.

"It's fun," said Mrs. Dawson. "So's Old Maid." She held up another box.

"We have Old Maid cards," said Ellen.

"How about a Parcheesi set?" said Mrs. Dawson, and when they turned it down she urged other games on them. Randall was glad when more customers came into the store and she left to wait on them.

The twins were not tall enough to see onto the counter, and they went back to the front of the store to study the different kinds of candy. The counter there had glass across the front that went almost to the floor.

Ellen and Randall continued to look at the assortment of games till Randall said, "Why don't we buy Ida Early a present?"

"I was thinking that same thing," said Ellen.

Neither of them had spoken of the incident in the schoolyard.

"We let her down," said Randall.

"Maybe."

"I haven't been able to think of anything else all day. What we did was cowardly."

"Oh, I don't know," said Ellen.

Randall guessed that she did know but wasn't ready to admit it. "We should have said something," he told her.

"I don't know if we could've stopped them."

"But we didn't even try," insisted Randall. "Of course, she could've stopped them by walking on!" He sounded as if he were angry at Ida, but he knew he was angry with himself.

"Maybe it's not her nature to walk on whenever anybody wants to talk," said Ellen. "Maybe she's lonely down deep. What do you think?"

"I think we should buy her a box of candy. She'd like it."

"No," said Ellen, "we'd wind up eating most of it. What about perfume?"

"*You'd* wind up using most of it!"

When Randall had given up on finding a gift for Ida, Ellen asked, "What about a checker board? Do you suppose she knows how to play checkers?"

"Why, I'd imagine she was once-upon-a-time the

champion checker player of the whole wide
world!" He was a bit ashamed of himself for doing
an imitation of Ida, but Ellen laughed. And at
least they had agreed on what to buy.

After the board and checkers had been pur-
chased, there was enough money left for an ice
cream cone for everyone. Partway home Randall
noticed that Dewey had not finished his; it was
dripping onto the road. "Eat your ice cream!" he
said.

"I'm saving a little for Ida."

"It'll melt," said Randall, and Dewey reluctantly licked the last of the cream. "I'll save the
cone part for her," he said.

Randall wondered what Ida would say when
they got home. Would she act as if nothing had
happened in the schoolyard, or would she be mad
with him and Ellen for not even admitting that
they knew her? He kept thinking of the hurt look
on her face. He'd glimpsed it at other times—at
the carnival when the man, Noon, had made such
ugly remarks, and once or twice when his aunts
had made snide comments. But on those occasions
the hurt expression was fleeting; in the schoolyard
it had lasted.

If only Dan Rogers hadn't started yelling at
Ida. And if Daisy Coker and Fay Edison hadn't
come along and made things worse. But Randall

knew that he was the one who'd failed Ida. Ellen had been there later, but he'd been in on the incident from the beginning. If he'd said something then like, "Hey, Dan, that's Ida Early you're talking to—she's our friend," or maybe just introduced them to each other, everything would have been different.

He couldn't erase the picture in his mind of Ida's expression as she left the schoolyard. It haunted him. He thought of nothing else until they were home.

Dewey ran into the house first. "Ida?" he called. "Ida, we're back!"

"We stayed in school the way we promised," called Clay, but there was no answer.

"She must be outside," said Dewey, going onto the back porch and calling, "Ida? Where are you, Ida?"

Clay went onto the porch too, and together they called for Ida as loudly as they could. But still there was no answer.

Changes

"Ida wouldn't leave us," said Dewey.

Randall was glad someone could be certain of it, but when the twins were out of earshot he said, "You know, she may be gone for good."

"Yes, I know," said Ellen. "She must have really been disappointed in us."

"*I'm* disappointed in us," said Randall, and he and Ellen talked for a long time about what had happened.

It was after dark when Mr. Sutton returned

home, and the twins greeted him with, "Ida's not here!" They said it at the same time.

"I know," said Mr. Sutton.

"Has she gone forever?" asked Clay.

"Of course not! She left word for me at work that she wouldn't be here tonight. I don't know what came up so suddenly. Somebody saw her hitchhiking on the road to Gainesville." Then he teased the twins. "Which one of you plans to cook supper for us?"

"We'd rather play tiddlywinks," said Dewey.

"All right, you play tiddlywinks," said Mr. Sutton, giving Dewey a playful swat. Then he turned to Ellen and Randall, who were studying at the table. "Be putting your homework aside," he said, "and let's see what we can do about something to eat."

They cleared away their books, and Randall set the table while Ellen poured a glass of milk for each place. Mr. Sutton fried country bacon that he called "streak o' lean," but he almost burned it. He said that it could be called "streak o' charcoal" this time. "Never mind, the gravy'll be good," he said, adding flour to the drippings in the skillet. "I should be able to make thickened gravy, wouldn't you think?" But when he poured milk into it, the mixture thickened too much. Even when he'd filled the skillet to the brim, the mixture still looked more like pudding than gravy. He dumped it into the bucket of scraps behind the stove. "Mayflower can have it for breakfast," he said. "Maybe she'll like my cooking!"

Randall looked into the cupboard. "Even if the gravy had been all right," he said, "there's no bread to eat with it."

Finally Ellen found string beans that Aunt Earnestine had canned during the summer. They were heated, and the rest of the supper consisted of soda crackers and sardines from a shelf in the pantry. During the meal Mr. Sutton said, "Probably there'll be other times Ida'll want to get away for a while." Winking at Randall, he added, "In which case, it might not be a bad idea if somebody here at least learned how to make biscuits!"

Ellen said, "Well, just because I'm the only girl doesn't mean it has to be me! Besides, I've heard that real chefs are—"

Clay interrupted her. "What're chefs?"

"Cooks at big eating places," said Ellen. "And they're nearly always men."

Mr. Sutton laughed. "Okay, okay! So Randall and I'll learn to make biscuits!"

In the morning Ida had not returned, and in the afternoon when the children got home from school Randall doubted she was there. Everything was too quiet. Usually, when she was home, she'd call out to them before they were halfway up the driveway. He opened the door, and Dewey squealed, "Ida!" She was sitting on the other side of the table, reading the paper. The twins dashed around the table and scrambled into her lap. "We're glad you're back!" said Dewey.

"Don't ever leave us again!" said Clay.

Randall thought that Ida looked different. Then he realized that she was wearing a new sweater. It was button-up, the same as her old one, but it was not as bulky and did not have patches on the elbows. And it was pink—very pale pink. She looked up at him and Ellen.

No one said anything for a moment. Then Randall said, "Howdy, Ida!" He tried to sound especially friendly, but he was afraid he'd overdone it and had sounded insincere instead.

"Hello," said Ida flatly. Usually she said "Howdy!" good and loud when she greeted anybody. Randall didn't recall ever hearing her say "hello" to anyone. She looked away after she'd spoken to him.

Ellen said, "Welcome home, Ida!"

"Thank you," said Ida, still with no feeling.

There was another silence. Randall studied the sad expression on Ida's face. Her eyes did not have their usual sparkle, and she looked as if she'd never smiled in her life. He decided it was her downcast expression that made more of a difference in her appearance than the sweater. At the same time, the sweater didn't seem right for her. It was too soft a color for someone as robust as Ida. Or maybe he'd just become accustomed to seeing her in the brown one. He was trying to think how to begin an apology about the schoolyard incident when Ellen said, "I like the new sweater. It's pretty."

"Thank you," said Ida, her voice still flat.

Randall then blurted out, "We're sorry about what happened at school."

"Yes, we are," said Ellen, "and if—"

Ida interrupted her. "Let's don't talk about it."

There was a brief silence again, and Randall expected the twins to ask what all this was about. Instead, Dewey asked Ida, "Will you read us the funnies?"

"Read us yesterday's too," said Clay. He added angrily, "Nobody else would read 'em to us."

Randall said, "You didn't ask for them till after you were in bed and the lamp was blown out."

Dewey said, "Ida would have read 'em to us, wouldn't you, Ida?"

"Yeah," said Clay. "I'll bet you could read in the dark, couldn't you, Ida?"

"Ida can do anything," said Dewey, flipping

through the newspaper to find the comics.

It was not until after she had read the comic strips to the twins and they'd climbed down from her lap that Ida stood up. No one had noticed till then that she was not wearing overalls. She had on a dress. It was a pale green one with dark green leaves printed on it. Dainty yellow flowers were sprinkled among the leaves. The dress hung loosely on her and was longer on one side than the other. Randall remembered how particular his mother had been in making certain that the hems of her dresses were always even. He looked again at Ida. He wondered where she'd found a dress big enough for her. Then he remembered that there was a small factory in Gainesville where dresses were made. So that was it: she'd gone there to buy the dress. She was trying to fix herself up, he knew, but that was silly. Why didn't she wear whatever suited her? Of course, he knew the answer. And if he'd had the guts to speak up yesterday, he told himself, nobody would have laughed at Ida about her clothes. He looked at her shoes and was glad that at least they were the same as they'd been. Though the thought crossed his mind that the brogans might not go with her dress and sweater.

In late afternoon Ida went over to the shelf near the icebox. "Time to do the milking," she said.

"I'll do the milking," said Randall. "I can take that job back if you'd like."

"I'll keep doing it," she said.

"But you're too dressed up," insisted Randall.

Ida took down the pail from its shelf. "Women milk cows wearing dresses all the time," she said.

"Cows wearing dresses?" said Clay.

Everybody laughed but Ida. "No, *women wearing dresses*," she said. She didn't smile, but she patted Clay on the head as she started outside.

"Now that's what I'd call *a good supper!*" said Mr. Sutton, pushing his chair back from the table. "You outdid yourself, Ida!"

"Thank you," said Ida, starting to clear the table. Randall and Ellen helped her. The twins and Mr. Sutton stayed at the table.

"Quite an improvement over last night, wouldn't you say, boys?" said Mr. Sutton.

"Last night was awful!" said Clay.

"Aw, now," said Mr. Sutton, "we did the best we could."

"Breakfast was awful too!" said Clay. "Was *that stuff* really oatmeal?"

Mr. Sutton laughed. "No, I think it was mule feed that was put on the pantry shelf by mistake. Maybe Ida'll show us how to make good oatmeal."

"She won't have to show us," said Clay. "She's

back now, and she'll make it for us. Won't you, Ida?"

"Sure," said Ida from across the room, not sounding at all enthusiastic about it. She stood over Mayflower's scrap bucket, scraping leftover mashed potatoes into it. She made little noise. Usually, when she was scraping out a dish, she'd bang the spoon against it, even tapping out a rhythm. Of course, she didn't always stand over the bucket. Sometimes when the contents of a pan or bowl were not to be saved for another meal she'd throw them into the bucket from halfway across the kitchen. Things like baked potatoes or biscuits were easy; Randall and Ellen had learned to throw them. But Ida could hurl other things as well. "A double backhand shot!" she'd said the night she'd thrown two squash halves over one shoulder and a helping of spaghetti over the other. And her specialty had been mashed potatoes. She could load them onto the big end of a mixing spoon or flapjack turner and flip them an amazing distance. They'd land with a plop in Mayflower's bucket. But now she stood over the bucket, scraping the potatoes into it as anyone else would have done. She was not herself, thought Randall, and it made him sad.

Mr. Sutton explained to the twins, "I mean that just in case we're ever on our own again, we should know more about cooking than we do." He added firmly, "I, for one, am going to learn!" When no one joined him in the resolution, he said, "Anyway, we mustn't take Ida for granted."

"What's *for granted*?" asked Dewey.

"It means we mustn't act as if Ida's been given to us. We hope she'll stay with us, but this is a free country and—well, who knows?—she might decide someday that she can't put up with us any longer." He looked at Ida as if he expected her to say something. When she didn't, he continued, "Or maybe some rich, handsome prince'll come riding out of the woods one day and grab her up and go galloping off to Nashville or someplace." The children laughed, but Ida didn't. Mr. Sutton looked puzzled. He had expected Ida to carry on with the joke.

Clay said, "I thought you said there weren't any real princes and princesses around here and that such things only happened in make-believe."

"Well, I was making believe," said Mr. Sutton.

"Anyway," said Clay, "no prince could grab Ida and take her away if she didn't want to go. Could they, Ida?"

"Not likely," agreed Ida.

Dewey said, "You'd grab his horse by the tail, with him sitting in the saddle, and sling 'em 'round and 'round, wouldn't you, Ida?"

"Plumb off the mountain," said Ida. She did not smile.

"Well," said Mr. Sutton, "if nobody likes my stories, run get a book and let's read a real one!"

Quickly Dewey fetched *Grimm's Fairy Tales*, and Mr. Sutton read aloud to the twins—and anyone else who cared to listen. Randall, putting away pots and pans after Ida had washed and Ellen wiped them, tried to make as little noise as possible. He liked hearing his father read aloud.

When the dishes were washed, Ellen brought out the checker board and put it on the table. "Here's a present!" she said.

"For us?" said Dewey. "What is it?"

"No," said Ellen. "It's for Ida."

"But what is it?" asked Clay.

"A checker board," said Randall. "Maybe we'll play something besides tiddlywinks around here for a while."

"But we don't know how to play checkers," said Dewey.

"We'll teach you," said Randall. "But it's Ida's board, and she gets to be first. Who you wanna play, Ida?"

"I'm going to bed," said Ida. "Let somebody else be first."

"You're not sick, are you?" asked Mr. Sutton.

"No, I'm not sick."

"If anything's wrong, I hope you'll let us try to help you."

"I'll be all right."

"You don't seem quite yourself," said Mr. Sutton. "In fact, you don't look quite yourself either." He looked surprised now, as if he had not seen her during supper. "Why, I knew something was different—you're not wearing overalls!" He waited for her to reply. When she said nothing he added hastily, "The dress looks nice. But why're you sprucing up so?"

"I just . . ." She hesitated before starting over. "Well, I just . . ." Her voice had quavered a bit, and Randall knew that she was embarrassed. He hoped his father wouldn't insist on knowing what was the matter. "I just figured it was time I tried to look a little better," Ida said at last.

Mr. Sutton smiled. "You've always looked fine to us. We want you to be happy; that's what we care about." When Ida said nothing, he added, "I'm glad you're not sick or anything."

As Ida started from the room, she said softly, "There's nothing wrong." She did not sound at all sure of it herself.

Checker Games
and the Curling Iron

One afternoon when Randall and the twins went down to the mailbox, there was a package for Ida. "Let's hurry back to the house and see what's in it!" said Dewey.

"But it's to Ida," said Randall.

"Yes, I know. But she'll show us."

Inside, Randall gave Ida the package. She put it on a chair and went ahead scraping carrots for supper. "Aren't you gonna open the package?" asked Clay.

"No."

"But don't you want to know what's in it?" he asked.

"I know what's in it," said Ida. Then she added, "Come on, let's go read Moon Mullins. We need something to make us laugh."

She read Moon Mullins and the other comics aloud, and Randall noticed that the twins laughed; she didn't. But that night at supper he saw what had been in the package. Instead of brogans, Ida was wearing a pair of women's shoes. They were made of black patent leather and had low heels and straps that fastened on the side. They reminded Randall of the ones worn by a lady tap dancer who'd put on a program at school last year. Ida hobbled when she walked in them as if they hurt her feet.

Every day afterward Ida wore the new shoes, although Randall believed they were too small for her. Finally she could walk in them without limping, and she wore them everywhere—even to the barn to do the milking.

After supper, whenever Mr. Sutton wasn't too tired, he played games with the twins or read to them until their bedtime. Recently he'd been teaching them to play checkers. Sometimes Randall would play too—and occasionally Ellen. Ida

Early went to bed as soon as the dishes were washed and put away. One night Mr. Sutton said, "Ida, it's not like you to turn in so early. Why don't you play checkers with us?"

"Some other time," said Ida, and she went ahead to her room.

The next night Mr. Sutton said, "Well, Clay and Dewey are about to get the hang of checkers, but they could still use a little coaching. How would it be, Ida, if I helped one of them and you helped the other?"

"I guess that'd be all right," said Ida, putting away the dishcloth. She sat down beside Dewey and gave him advice during the game. Dewey won. Next she helped Clay, and Clay won. It was the beginning of checker sessions that Mr. Sutton called "nightly attempts to beat Ida." Nobody succeeded. Several times Randall believed he was about to win a game only to find that he'd been trapped. Ida would make a clever move and wipe his men off the board.

One evening while a game was under way Ellen came into the room with a curling iron. "I ran across this today in Mamma's things," she said. "I believe I'll curl my hair." She looked at her father as if she expected him to say, "No, you can't do that!"

"Your hair looks fine to me the way it is," he

said. "But if you've got the patience to try curling it, just be careful that you don't get the iron too hot and burn yourself."

"I'll be careful," said Ellen, hurrying to put the iron on the stove.

Checker games continued, and when the twins' bedtime came, Dewey said, "Ida, how come you don't laugh when you win?"

"Yeah," said Clay. "You used to laugh lots."

"Just haven't had much notion to, I guess," said Ida, folding up the board. "But maybe I'll get back in the habit." She smiled at Randall. He wished he could think of some way to cheer her up.

"How does it look?" asked Ellen, coming near the big Alladin lamp in the center of the room. She had finished trying to curl her hair.

Clay said, "It looks curly."

"That's the way it's supposed to look."

"Turn around," said Mr. Sutton, "and let's see it in the back."

Ellen turned around. "Does it bush out too much?" she asked.

"Maybe just a little," said Mr. Sutton. "But it'll settle down." He reached out and pulled her to him. "I'm not sure that I'm ready for you to be so grown-up, but then, I guess there's no stopping you." He kissed her and added, "You look pretty."

Two days later, when the children came home

from school, Ida's hair had been curled. Randall saw the curling iron on the back of the stove.

No two strands of Ida's hair seemed to go in the same direction. Clumps of it stood out from her head as if they'd been wired. Strands drooped; others stood straight up. There was one lock that was Z-shaped. Even sadder-looking was Ida's expression. Randall felt sorry for her. He thought of the day Ida had arrived and how her hair had reminded him of the scarecrow's. But since then he'd grown to like it. The shaggy-mop effect might not look nice on all women, but it had been right for Ida. In the same way, her overalls and brogans had looked more appropriate than the dress and shoes she wore now. Possibly he'd become accustomed to seeing her in the new outfit. But he doubted he'd ever get used to the startling change in her appearance made by the curling iron.

Neither he nor Ellen said anything when they looked at Ida, and even the twins were quiet for a moment. Then Dewey said, "Maybe it'll look better when it settles down."

Ida lifted him off the floor and gave him a hug.

The Letter

"Where are the biscuits?" asked Dewey. The children had just returned from school and were in the kitchen.

"In the cupboard," said Ida, who was putting a jigsaw puzzle together at the table.

"But they don't have jam and peanut butter on them," complained Clay.

"Spread them yourselves," said Ida. She put the last piece into the puzzle and went over to the twins. "You must learn to do things on your own."

"Why," asked Clay, "if you'll do them for us?"

"That's just it. I won't always be here to do them for you. And you'd be better off, anyway, not to depend on me." But all the while, she was spreading jam and peanut butter for them.

"If you go off," said Clay, "I'm going with you."

Dewey said, "Ida won't go away, will you, Ida?"

Ida handed him a biscuit. "I can't stay one place forever. I get restless."

"I get restless too," said Clay. "We'll go with you, won't we, Dewey?"

"Can Daddy go?" asked Dewey. "And Randall and Ellen?"

"Nope," said Ida, "just me. When the time comes, I'll be gone—*swoosh!*—like a wild goose."

Dewey said, "You wouldn't go without telling us good-bye, would you?"

"I wouldn't go if I had to say good-bye," said Ida. "I believe in '*Howdy!*' 'Good-bye' ain't for me." She closed the cupboard door and asked the twins if they'd like to go for a walk in the woods.

Clay and Dewey said yes, they wanted to go; they always liked to walk with Ida. After they'd gone, Randall and Ellen talked. "Ida's gonna leave any day now," said Randall.

"Yes, I believe she's been trying to tell us without coming right out and saying so."

"I wish she had let us really apologize to her," said Randall.

"Me too."

"I know what let's do," said Randall. "Let's write her a letter telling her how sorry we are. I'll hide it in her knapsack, and she'll come across it after she's gone. Then when she reads it, maybe she won't hate us as much."

"I don't think she hates us," said Ellen. "But at least she'll know we really care. Let's write the letter."

Randall turned to a fresh piece of paper in his notebook and asked, "What should we say first?"

"How about, 'Wherever you are when you find this, you can be sure that we are missing you'?"

" 'And wishing you were back with us,' " said Randall, writing the sentence.

Ellen suggested that next they say, " 'We are ashamed of the way we let our classmates tease you in the schoolyard.' "

" 'And we will never again fail to come to the aid of a friend,' " added Randall.

"But Ida's more than a friend," said Ellen. "She's more like part of the family."

"Then you think of what to say."

Ellen cupped her chin in her hands and thought for a long time. "How about, 'We will never again fail to come to the aid of someone we love'?"

Randall looked up. He didn't say anything for a moment. "Yeah," he said at last. "I've never thought of it, but yeah, you're right." He wrote the sentence. Then they said again how sorry they were that they'd let her down, and they closed the letter with, "If you will forgive us we will be your true friends forever." Both of them signed it.

In Ida's room Randall looked around for her knapsack. It was on a chair in the corner, and he could tell from the way it bulged that something was already in it. It was sneaky, he knew, to open it, and he told himself that he'd just slide the letter underneath whatever was there. But when he found that it was Ida's overalls that were in the knapsack, he unfastened the bib pocket of them and put the letter there. He'd bet that one day she'd wear the overalls again, and he could imagine her surprise when she'd start to put a bag of tobacco into the pocket and find the letter.

Randall left Ida's room and went outside. He took down a rope from a peg in the toolshed and went to the clearing just beyond the woodpile. There he made a noose in the end of the rope and tried using it as a lasso. He tried to lasso the chopping block for a long time but succeeded only when he stood directly over it. When he saw Ida and the twins returning from their walk, he stopped and took a load of wood to the house. Then he went back to the yard and tried for a long time to lasso a fence post.

"What're you doing with a rope?" asked Ida, when she came along with the milking bucket. "Who're you gonna tie up?"

Randall laughed. "Nobody. I'm trying to turn it into a lasso, but I'm not doing very well. I'm supposed to be a cowboy in a program at school on Friday." He looked at Ida. "I don't suppose you know how to use a lasso?" If she were the old Ida, he imagined she'd have said that she'd been in rodeos all over the world, or something like that, whether she knew how to use a rope or not. But now that she was wearing a dress and shoes with straps on them and had strange-looking curls in her hair, she never got enthusiastic about anything.

"Yes, I know a little about using a lasso," she said. "Here, loop the rope this way, it's easier." She showed him how to do the loops as she talked. Then she asked, "What would you like me to lasso?"

"I've been trying to put the noose over that corner post on Mayflower's pen for the last half-hour."

Before he'd finished saying it, Ida had thrown

the rope over the post and tightened the noose.

Randall ran to the post and took the rope off. "Was that just luck?" he asked while she whirled the rope around her as if it were a hoop. "Or can you do it again?"

Ida threw the noose over the post again as if it were the easiest thing in the world. "Anything else?" she asked.

Randall looked around for a suitable target. "Maybe that washtub over on the laundry bench."

"The big 'un or the little 'un?" asked Ida. "Or both?" Without waiting for an answer, she threw out the rope and put it around both tubs. They clanked loudly when they were pulled together.

"That took 'em by surprise!" said Randall. "What about that old sawhorse up there? Pretend it's a calf!"

"Find me another rope, and I'll tie that 'calf' up for you!"

Randall hurried to the toolshed and brought back ropes that had once been used for plow lines.

"The sawhorse, huh?" said Ida, and in a flash she put a rope around it. She pulled the sawhorse onto its side and quickly put another rope around it—and then another. "And now, ladies and gentlemen," she said, as if she were performing on a stage, "I'll lasso a moving target."

"Where?" asked Randall excitedly.

"*You!*" said Ida. "Strike out running and see if you can get away from me!"

Randall dashed away, and when he believed he was completely out of Ida's reach, the rope dropped over him, pinning his arms to his sides. Immediately another rope tied his feet together, and he couldn't move. "That's amazing!" he said while Ida was untying him. "I want to learn."

"It takes a while," said Ida. "But I'll give you a few pointers."

Randall practiced with a rope while Ida did the milking, but he doubted he'd ever get the knack of it. Then he realized that he wasn't seriously concentrating on it; thoughts were coming into his mind that were more important to him than learning to use a lasso. He'd been trying to think of a way to prove to Ida that he was not ashamed of her, and maybe this was it: he'd ask her to be on the program with him. When she came along back from the barn, he said, "Ida, would you come to the program at school on Friday?"

"Thank you," she said, "but I'd better not. It'd be interesting to see you being a cowboy, but—"

Randall interrupted her. "No, I mean would you be on the program and do some rope tricks and lassoing?"

Ida grinned, and her eyes sparkled. "Of course I

will!" she said. Then her grin disappeared and she shook her head. "No. But thanks all the same."

"Please, won't you be on the program?" said Randall. "Our room's in charge of it, and it's about the Old West, and—well, you'd be great." He detected a gleam in her eye, and he hurried on. "There'll be lots of folks there. Some of 'em'll be the ones who hollered at you that time you passed along the schoolyard." He hadn't meant to remind her of the incident. He looked at her, wondering if she'd be upset.

She smiled. "I wouldn't mind showing them what I can do!" she said.

"When my part on the program comes up," said Randall, "everybody'll be thinking, 'Well, he's not gonna do anything special.' Then I'll introduce you, and you can dazzle 'em with rope tricks!"

Ida laughed. "Yeah, I could do that all right!"

"You mean you'll come?"

"I mean I'll think about it." She started toward the house. "Maybe I'll be there on Friday. Just *maybe.*"

Rope Tricks

The theme of the program was "The Old West."
Milly Jordan had thought of it when Mrs. Long,
the sixth-grade teacher, had asked for ideas. The
upper elementary and high-school grades met
once a month for an assembly, and this was the
first time the sixth grade had been asked to put on
the program. Naturally, everyone wanted it to be
good. Because Milly had thought of the theme,
Mrs. Long had said that she could be Program
Chairman.

On Friday, just after lunch, Randall and J.C. hurried into the dressing room at the side of the stage. Everyone else was already there. Randall and J.C. had waited out front for Ida, but she had not shown up. Maybe she was just running late, Randall told himself; there was still time. But Ida was not there when the bell rang, which meant that the audience would soon be filing into the auditorium.

Mr. Carlisle, the principal, came into the room. "It's almost time to start," he said. "Is everything all set?"

"Yes, sir, I think so," said Milly.

"Where's Mrs. Long?"

"She's out front with the rest of us," said Milly.

"The *rest of us*!" said Mr. Carlisle, laughing.

"I mean the ones in the sixth grade who're not on the program."

Mr. Carlisle laughed more, but he stopped abruptly. Pointing toward the corner, near the door to the stage, he gasped, "What's that?"

"It's a bear," said Milly as if Mr. Carlisle didn't really know a grown bear when he saw one.

"But when you told me about that part of the program, I didn't know you meant *live* animals!" He sounded upset.

Milly answered calmly, "The bear's the only live one."

Mr. Carlisle looked at the boys who were sitting on the floor. "I thought it was *all* to be like whoever-that-is wearing the paper sack over his head with a dog's face on it."

"It's supposed to be a coyote's face," said Milly. She turned to Randall. "I told Vivian that coyotes didn't have floppy ears." Vivian was their classmate who had done the artwork. Turning back to Mr. Carlisle, Milly said, "And it's Timmy Rico who's wearing it. He's going to pretend to bark at the moon." Randall had helped Milly dangle a big yellow balloon from the ceiling of the stage; it was the moon. They'd put it just above the covered wagon. The covered wagon was made of big pieces of pasteboard glued together and nailed to an old bookshelf. Vivian had painted what looked like a wagon body and wheels onto the pieces of pasteboard. An old sheet had been put across the top; it was the cover of the covered wagon. The effect of it was not as real as that of the campfire nearby—a red lantern with chunks of wood stacked around it. The glow of the lantern made it look as if the pieces of wood were burning.

Milly looked out the door to the auditorium. "They're not all in yet," she said. Then she explained to Mr. Carlisle, "Jeff and Roger are to be a buffalo. They don't look too much like one now, but when they go out on the stage they'll have a brown blanket over them all scrunched up in the middle."

Roger said, " 'Cept it ain't brown."

"And it ain't a blanket," added Jeff. "It's an old yellow bedspread. Mamma said that's all we had that was wore-out enough to bring."

"Never mind! Never mind!" said Mr. Carlisle, looking at the bear again.

The bear was owned by Mr. Paul Harley, who had a store out in the country. Almost every year he or one of his sons would catch a cub, and they'd tame it and train it and keep it till somebody came along who wanted to buy a bear. Then they'd sell it and catch another one. People from miles around knew Mr. Harley's store because there was nearly always a bear in the cage out front. Mr. Harley was Milly's uncle; Randall knew that was how she'd been lucky enough to get a real wild animal for the program. It was the biggest bear that Randall had ever seen and did not look at all playful, like a cub. Usually the Harleys sold their bears before they were grown, but maybe nobody had come along who'd wanted this one.

Mr. Harley's grown son, Wilbur, had brought the bear today. They were almost the same size, Wilbur and the bear, but Wilbur looked plenty strong enough to control any animal. His face alone, with squinty eyes peering out from behind a matted beard, would scare them, thought Randall. Even so, he was glad that Wilbur appeared to have a good hold on the rope that was tied to the collar around the bear's neck.

Mr. Carlisle peeked out the door to the auditorium. "Well, it looks as if everybody's in place; we'd better begin. I'll go out and make a few announcements and then turn the program over to you." He looked at the bear then as if he were only now realizing that he must walk past it to go onto the stage. He looked at Wilbur and then at the bear, then back at Wilbur. "Can you hold on to the bear all right?" he asked.

"He ain't never got away from me," growled Wilbur.

"And the muzzle'll stay in place?"

"It ain't never come off," said Wilbur. The muzzle over the bear's snout made the beast look safe, thought Randall, but its paws could be deadly too. They could tear someone apart.

Mr. Carlisle drew in a deep breath and walked past Wilbur and the bear. When he was on the other side of them, he pulled open the door to the stage. With the door between him and the bear, he spoke to Wilbur again. "You can understand why I have to be careful," he said. "I mean, the bear's not apt to hurt anyone, is he?"

"Just schoolteachers," said Wilbur. The children

laughed, but Mr. Carlisle did not. He hurried onto the stage.

After the announcements Milly went out and told the audience how the program, called "The Old West," was divided into three parts. She said, "The first part is 'Music of the Old West.' And here they are, the Old West singers and dancers!"

Randall's classmates who were on that part of the program went onto the stage and sat around the campfire. The girls sang "I Want to Be a Cowboy's Sweetheart." The boys sang "Whoopee Ti Yi Yo, Git Along Little Doggies." Then they all did a square dance. Randall couldn't enjoy the music for worrying that Ida Early had not arrived. Of course, she'd said only, "Maybe," but still, he'd expected her to come.

When the dance ended, Randall heard Milly telling the audience that the next part of the program was "People of the Old West." Suddenly he felt ill. It would soon be time for him to go onstage. He was to do nothing more than walk out, twirling a rope—unless Ida had shown up, in which case he was to have introduced her. Yet his stomach was queasy, and he believed his legs were going to give way beneath him. It was stagefright, he knew. He told himself he was being silly, but that didn't help. He'd been on programs when only two or three grades got together, but this would be the first time he'd ever been on a stage in front of a crowd.

The first of the "people of the Old West" to go out was J. C. He walked across the stage carrying a small black satchel and was supposed to be a frontier doctor. He was followed by a preacher: Cal Adams, with a Bible tucked under his arm. Then there was Nell Johnson. She wore an apron over her dress, had on a sunbonnet, and carried a skillet with a flapjack in it. She flipped the flapjack into the air as she walked and was supposed to be a frontier housewife. The "flapjack" was only a round pot holder, but it looked like a flapjack.

Joe Blakley was a sheriff and Dan Rogers a gunslinger. They walked onto the stage, drew cap pistols from holsters, and fired noisily at each other. When both of them fell dead, the audience cheered. Randall, watching from the doorway, enjoyed it till he realized again that he had to go out there.

"And now," announced Milly, "here he is—The Cowboy!"

Randall put on the wide-brim hat that Mrs. Long had brought for him to wear and made his way onto the stage. He felt weak, and he knew that he wobbled a bit. A rope dangled from one arm, but he did not attempt to twirl it; it was an effort just to walk. An eighth grader yelled, "We see the hat—where's the cowboy?"

Randall had known that the hat was too big for him, but his ears had held it up till the heckling remark was made. At that point the hat dropped down over his face. There were snickers from the audience. Randall felt his face grow hot, and when he pushed the hat up far enough to see out, his brow was wet with perspiration. It was then that he saw Ida. She stood among some of the mothers in back who had come to watch the program. Anyone might have mistaken her for one of them except that none of the others was holding an armful of ropes.

Immediately Randall forgot his stagefright. Throwing his hat off, he yelled, "Hey, Ida, come up here! I need you!"

Ida strolled down the aisle. A few people in the audience snickered. Maybe they laughed because of the ropes, thought Randall; nothing else about her was funny. The dress, although it still hung down farther on one side than the other, was no different from the dresses many women wore. The shoes, he had to admit, were a little different, especially now that she was leaving the straps unfastened. The buckles flapped against her ankles. And her hair, since she'd taken the curling iron to it, was more unkempt than ever. But anyone who laughed at her wasn't seeing the real Ida, the one who mattered, thought Randall. He held out his hand to her when she started up the steps at the front of the stage.

Randall said to the audience, "This is my friend, Ida Early, and she's gonna do some rope tricks for you like they used to do in the Old West."

Casey Stallings, a seventh-grade boy sitting on the center aisle near the front, waved an arm in the air and called, "Hey, see if you can rope me!" In a flash, Ida threw out a rope and looped it around Casey's arm that he was waving. "No!" he yelled. "I didn't mean it! I didn't mean it!"

"Shouldn't say what you don't mean!" said Ida, tugging at the rope firmly so that Casey couldn't loosen it. She put just enough pressure on it to make him move forward. He stumbled up the steps and onto the stage, and everyone in the auditorium laughed.

"What else you want roped?" asked Ida as she unfastened the rope from around Casey's wrist.

"How about that chair over there?" asked Randall, and Ida put a rope around the chair.

Casey edged away. He slunk off the stage and up the aisle. He was almost at his seat when Ida threw out a rope and looped it around his waist. She pulled him backwards down the aisle and up onto the stage, with everyone enjoying it but Casey.

Ida did other tricks, appearing to be concentrating solely on twirling the rope or throwing it wherever Randall suggested, but each time Casey tried to get away she'd throw out a rope and snag him. And each time she pulled him back. It looked as if it had been planned, and everybody enjoyed it. Mr. Carlisle laughed more than anyone else, and finally even Casey was laughing.

Before the rope tricks ended, Ida had put a noose over the piano and its bench, two chairs, a speaker's stand, and every chunk of wood on the campfire without upsetting the lantern. She had lassoed almost everything on the stage except Mr. Carlisle. Randall thought it might be interesting for her to put a rope around him too, but he didn't suggest it.

When the roping was over, the audience cheered loudly. Ida held one of Casey's arms in the air as if he were a champion before sending him back to his place. Then she held up one of Randall's arms and together they took a bow.

Mr. Carlisle invited Ida to have a chair onstage beside him for the rest of the program. Randall stopped with Joe Blakley back of the covered wagon to watch "Part Three: Animals of the Old West."

The buffalo was introduced first, and Roger, pretending to be the front half, and Jeff, the last half, with the bedspread over them, trotted around the stage twice and then off. Next, Timmy Rico came out as the coyote. He sniffed about the campfire and then, on seeing the balloon moon, sat back on his heels and howled piercingly. At that moment Joe reached over the top of the covered wagon and stuck a pin in the balloon. The crowd laughed uproariously, but Timmy, the coyote, did not think it was funny. He left the stage in a huff.

"Now," said Milly excitedly, "we're about to have the best part of all. Here comes my Cousin Wilbur and a bear!"

Wilbur and the bear lumbered onto the center of the stage. "Set down!" said Wilbur, and the bear sat down.

"Now stan' up!" ordered Wilbur, and the bear reared up on his back legs.

A high-school boy yelled, "Hey, which one's Cousin Wilbur?"

Randall decided later that it had been the loud outburst of laughter that had upset the bear. And the remark itself had upset Wilbur, making him just mad enough to slacken his attention. Randall had read that wild animals can sense it when a handler's concentration flicks off even for a second. The bear shook its head so ferociously that the muzzle went flying off to the side. At the same time, the bear lunged forward. Wilbur, thrown off balance, lost his hold on the rope and went reeling backwards. He crashed through the middle section of the covered wagon and onto the floor. The bear moved swiftly toward the front of the stage, and people in the audience began screaming. Students near the front scampered to get away.

The bear went to the edge of the stage. "Come back here!" yelled Wilbur, struggling to get to his feet, but the bear jumped from the stage onto the floor of the auditorium.

Daisy Coker, in the middle of the second row, tried to climb over the seat in front of her in order to get away quicker. Her shoe caught on the armrest, and she sprawled on the floor. There was nobody to give her a hand as everyone who'd been near her had escaped.

The bear leaped toward her, snarling fiercely, with its front legs outstretched. It was only inches from her. Daisy, shielding her face with her hands, screamed. Suddenly a rope dropped over the bear and pinned its front legs to its sides. Ida tugged frantically at the other end of the rope. Randall rushed to her side, and together they pulled the bear back far enough for Daisy to get away. Then Ida put another rope around the bear, and then another. Soon there were so many ropes around it, pulled securely, that it looked like a furry crate tied up for shipment. Ida even put a rope around its mouth and held it shut till Wilbur could replace the muzzle.

Finally, when the bear had been removed to Wilbur's pickup truck, everyone quieted down. Mr. Carlisle, appearing near collapse, said, "I think we'd better let that be enough program."

"Yes, sir," said Milly. "That's the end of it, anyway."

Mr. Carlisle asked the audience, "What do you think? Shouldn't we give a big hand to Miss Ida Early?" At that, the auditorium almost exploded; there was loud applause, foot-stomping, catcalling, shouting, and whistling.

Ida went out to the middle of the stage and took a deep bow. Her eyes sparkled and she grinned at the audience as the cheering continued. During her struggles to pull the bear away from Daisy, one of her shoes had come off. Also, a sleeve of her dress had ripped at the shoulder. The sleeve, hanging now by long threads, dropped down below her wrist, but it didn't bother her. Nor did the shoe; she held it in her hand as she walked offstage, waving to the audience one last time.

At home, the twins wanted to hear the story over and over about Ida lassoing the bear. Randall noticed that the story got better each time Ida told it. She added details here and there to make it all seem even more exciting than it had been. When finally the twins went outside to play, Randall and Ellen chatted with Ida about the program.

"You ought've heard my friends talking about you afterward!" said Randall. "They all wish you'd teach them to use a rope."

"Did they recognize me?" asked Ida. "I mean, did they know I was the one they'd made fun of that time?"

"They didn't till Dan Rogers suddenly realized it. Nobody would believe him till I told them it was true."

Ellen said, "You know, it's *something* the way things turn out! You saved Daisy Coker's life today, and she's the one in the schoolyard who yelled at you the most."

"Was *that* who that was?" said Ida. She was quiet for a moment. "Well, I didn't recognize her either . . . or I might not have been in such a hurry to stop that bear!" At that, she and Ellen and Randall laughed together so loud that the twins came running inside to see what had happened.

The Departure

The first day of October was the day after the program at school. Somehow Randall knew Ida was not there before he even walked into the house that afternoon. He couldn't explain why he felt the way he did. He only knew that it would be like Ida, if she was planning to go away, to leave after something special had happened instead of at an ordinary time. And yesterday had been special all right. He hated to think of Ida not being at home, but at the same time it shouldn't be a real surprise to anyone. She'd tried to prepare the family for getting along without her.

He looked in Ida's room. Her knapsack was gone, as he'd known it would be, and he went back to the kitchen. The twins were spreading peanut butter and jelly on biscuits that had been put in the cupboard.

"Ida's left us," said Randall.

"She'll be back," said Clay, sounding certain of it. Dewey was sure of it too, and all afternoon the twins insisted that Ida would be home any minute. They made up things she might be doing. "I'll bet she's gone to the drugstore and is eating ice cream right now," said Clay.

"Yes," agreed Dewey. "And then she'll buy us a jawbreaker apiece and come straight home. She'll buy a yellow one for you and a red one for me."

"No, I want the red one," said Clay.

Randall said, "Will you cut it out? Ida's gone."

The twins were quiet for a few minutes. Then Dewey said, "I know where Ida is! She's at that store where old men play checkers around the stove."

"Yeah," said Clay, "that's it! I'll bet she's beating them every one!"

Later they had another idea about where Ida

had gone. "She probably went out to Harley's store to make sure the bear's all right," said Dewey.

"That's it," said Clay. "She's there right now, patting the bear on the head and making friends with it!"

"She may bring it home with her," said Dewey.

Nothing Randall or Ellen said could convince the twins that Ida would not return. After supper Mr. Sutton tried. "Remember, she told us that someday she'd be gone."

"Like a wild goose!" said Clay. "But I don't believe she meant it."

"Yes, I think she meant it," said Mr. Sutton. "Some people are like that and have to keep moving." He pulled the twins onto his lap. "What do you say that instead of being sad, we try to be happy that we had Ida with us for as long as we did?"

The twins slid down from his lap. "Come on, Dewey," said Clay, "let's go onto the porch and see if we see Ida coming."

Mr. Sutton shook his head as they walked out. Then he said, "I'd better write your Aunt Earnestine and ask if she'll come help us out again."

"Couldn't we manage without her?" asked Randall.

"Yes, please, couldn't we?" said Ellen.

134

"The two of you can look after yourselves, but Dewey and Clay need a little help along. And there's cooking and housecleaning to do."

"We'll do the work," said Ellen.

"And we'll keep an eye on the twins," promised Randall.

Dewey and Clay came back into the room, and Mr. Sutton put an arm around them. "Do you think we can get along by ourselves, or should I send for Aunt Earnestine?"

"Send for Ida Early," said Dewey. "We want her back."

"All of us want Ida Early back," Mr. Sutton said.

"Don't send for Aunt Earnestine," said Clay. "She's mean."

"No, she's not mean," said Mr. Sutton. "She's just a little stern, and she's cross sometimes."

"She's mean," insisted Clay.

Mr. Sutton pushed back in his chair. "Maybe we *would* be happier if we tried it on our own."

"We can do it," said Ellen. "I'll cook if Randall will do the dishes."

"And we could all pitch in on the housecleaning," said her father. "If each one of us did our part to keep things in order it shouldn't be too bad. I can do some of the cooking."

"We can help too," said Dewey.

"Sure you can," said Mr. Sutton. "You'll both have to be big boys now and not get into a lot of mischief, all right?"

"We'll shake hands on it," said Clay, holding out his hand to his father. Dewey held out his hand too.

Mr. Sutton shook hands solemnly with Clay and Dewey and then leaned over and gave both of them a kiss on the forehead.

"We've struck us another bargain," said Dewey as he and Clay went in search of the tiddlywinks board. But later in the evening they cried because Ida was not there to put them to bed. Randall tucked the cover around them. He tried to think of a funny story to tell them, but none came to mind. "If it would do any good," he said, "I'd cry too."

The family managed to get along, but it was not like the good times when Ida was there. Ellen tried, but she was not a very good cook, and she knew how to prepare only three dishes: scrambled eggs, stew, and macaroni with cheese. Mr. Sutton helped, but he'd been especially busy at the lumberyard during October and had not been at home to do much of the cooking. November had started out in the same way. Also, Mr. Sutton had never done much in the kitchen himself. However, he became enthusiastic about improving his skills, and the family looked forward to meals that he prepared. When he wasn't there, they ate scrambled eggs, stew, or macaroni with cheese.

The children were careful not to complain about anything lest their father decide that Aunt Earnestine should come back after all. But they did sorely miss Ida Early. Randall knew that it was far more than her good cooking that made the difference; it was Ida herself.

One afternoon Randall sat at the kitchen table. His books were spread out in front of him, but he wasn't really studying. J. C. came in. If he had knocked or called out, Randall hadn't heard him. "Say," said J. C., "are you in a daze or something?"

"Oh, howdy, J. C.! I didn't know you were here."

"What were you thinking about so serious?"

"I was thinking about Ida Early. I wonder what's become of her."

"Didn't I tell you?" said J. C. "Jasper thought he saw her."

"I didn't know Jasper even knew her," said Randall. Jasper was J. C.'s cousin. He drove a taxi in Atlanta but came to the mountains every now and then to visit relatives.

"Yeah, he was at the carnival the time she showed up that fellow Noon in throwing baseballs."

"But where's he seen her since then?"

"In Atlanta. Out at Candler Field."

"The airfield? What was she doing?"

"Selling hot dogs and hamburgers at a stand just outside the terminal. He saw her when he was driving off; at least, he believed it was her."

Ellen called from her room, "I see Mr. Askew." Mr. Askew was the mail carrier.

"Is he stopping?" asked Randall.

"Yes, he's leaving something."

"Okay, I'll go see what it is," said Randall, and he and J. C. walked down to the mailbox.

There was a letter addressed to Mr. Sutton. "I'll bet it's from Ida Early," said Randall.

"Does it have a return address?" asked J. C.

"No, but it's postmarked Atlanta."

"Maybe that's why you were thinking about her so strong a while ago. Maybe there were thought waves going around in the air because her letter was almost here." J. C. was a big believer in thought waves.

"I don't know what it was," said Randall, "but something made me think of her more than ever."

Ellen and the twins also believed the letter was from Ida, and all four children were at the door when their father returned home.

"No," he said when he'd opened the letter, "it's not from Ida. It's from your Aunt Earnestine."

Randall agreed with Clay, who said disgustedly, "Why couldn't it have been from Ida?"

"Cheer up!" said Mr. Sutton when he'd read the letter. "Kathy Alice may come to see you!" All the children groaned. "Earnestine wants to meet your Aunt Myrtle and Uncle Ross and Kathy Alice here on Thanksgiving Day."

"Tell her we won't be home," said Ellen.

"Where will we be?" asked Dewey.

"Anywhere except here," said Ellen, "if they're coming to see us."

"Right!" said Randall.

"Now, be ashamed!" scolded Mr. Sutton, but he was smiling. "Of course, we'll be glad to see them even though I'm sure the trip is mainly to see what all we're doing wrong."

Randall said, "And it means Aunt Earnestine's gonna decide to stay and manage us."

Mr. Sutton said, "Yes, it probably does. But maybe we need her. You and Ellen are having to work too hard. I want you to have more time to play and visit your friends and enjoy being young."

Randall hated to think of Aunt Earnestine being put back in charge of the household. It was true that he'd had more work to do since Ida had been gone. But Aunt Earnestine wouldn't take over any of his chores outside—drawing water, milking, even sometimes chopping wood and hauling it to the woodbox in the kitchen—the way Ida did. And inside, he and Ellen would have as many chores as ever, whether Aunt Earnestine was there or not. Only Aunt Earnestine would fuss at them if they didn't work fast and do everything her way.

As he often did, Randall thought of Ida and wished she were there. He smiled when he recalled the rope tricks she'd done and the way she'd tied up the bear. That had been six weeks ago, but it was still talked about every day at school. Randall could see Ida, as clearly as if he were watching a motion picture of her, walking off the stage with one shoe on and the other in her hand, grinning, and waving to the cheering crowd. He was glad to have that picture in his mind: Ida triumphant; Ida in high spirits.

Randall and Ellen tried to convince their father that they could continue to look after the house and the twins, that it wasn't too much work for them.

"We'll see," said Mr. Sutton, and Randall suspected that "we'll see" in this instance meant Aunt Earnestine would move back in with them. It would be awful, he knew.

Almost Thanksgiving

Mrs. Broe, at a farm down the mountain, raised turkeys, and Mr. Sutton had asked her to reserve a nice one for him. The weekend before Thanksgiving, on Saturday afternoon, Randall and the twins walked to the farm to fetch the turkey home.

At the shed where the turkeys were penned up, Mrs. Broe said, "They're all about the same size. Take your choice."

Dewey pointed at a large tom. "I like that one," he said.

"This 'un?" asked Mrs. Broe, reaching for the turkey that was pecking at her shoelace.

"No," said Clay, "let's take the one in the corner."

Randall settled it: "We'll take the one you pick out for us."

Mrs. Broe picked up the one at her feet. "This should make a fine Thanksgiving Day feast for you!" She had Randall hold it while she tied its feet together with a piece of twine. "Now," she explained, "if you turned it loose it couldn't go far."

Clay and Dewey chatted with the turkey on the way home. It made a contented gurgling noise as if it were talking back to them.

When they were home, Randall untied the turkey's feet and put it in the henhouse. It spread its tail and gave a loud gobble. Then it stood quietly and let the twins pat it. "Come on," said Randall. "Let's go inside." Reluctantly the twins followed him into the house.

Mr. Sutton was in the kitchen. "Is the gobbler a good one?" he asked.

"Good and heavy!" said Randall. "I'd hate to've toted it another mile!"

Dewey said, "Maybe we ought to just keep it around for a while."

"Yes," said Clay, "let's let it grow some more."

"Oh, no!" said Mr. Sutton. "Don't start that! It's our company dinner for Thursday. We've got too many chickens around here that can't be put in the pot because they're your pets. So in the interest of us having an extra-special Thanksgiving dinner, *please* don't make a pet of the turkey!"

The twins didn't make any promise about it, and Randall could imagine they'd come up with a way to spare the turkey. He was trying to think what it might be when suddenly there was a loud noise outside.

"What in the world?" asked Ellen, who had just come into the room.

"A motorcycle out on the road," Mr. Sutton said.

Randall looked out the window. "Only it's not on the road. It's coming up our driveway." By then the noise was so loud that no one could be heard above it.

The motorcycle circled around the house and stopped in the backyard. There were two people on it, and one of them, the passenger, got off. The driver raced the motor—*vroom*—and roared out of the yard. *Vroom! Vroom!* The other person—tall, and wearing boots, riding pants, leather jacket, and an aviator's cap with goggles—walked up the steps, across the back porch, and into the kitchen. Randall held the door open and stood back. The caller threw off the goggles and cap.

"Ida Early!" squealed Ellen, running to her.

"No other!" said Ida with a big grin. "How's everybody?"

"Everybody's fine!" said Mr. Sutton. He went over and shook hands with her. "All of us are happy to see you."

Ida took off her jacket and, without turning her head, threw it across the room. It landed on a peg of the hatrack. "I've been down in Atlanta for a while," she said, "but I missed my *true friends*." She looked straight at Ellen and Randall. "In fact, I missed all my friends." She picked up Clay in one arm and Dewey in the other. "So I decided it might be a good idea to come back."

"You decided right!" said Mr. Sutton. He went across to the cookstove and added a chunk of wood to the fire in it.

"So I told 'em at the airfield they'd have to get along without me."

Clay and Dewey patted Ida lovingly on the head. Her hair had been cut short again and had a fresh, windblown look. "What were you doing at the airfield?" asked Clay.

"Oh, not much of anything," said Ida, and Clay looked disappointed until she added, "I just did stunts for 'em whenever they put on air shows. But to tell you the truth, I was getting a little bit bored walking around on the wings of airplanes, jumping from one to another while they were flying way up high, and that sort of thing." She gave Clay and Dewey a kiss on the cheek and put them down. "I was ready for something more exciting."

"Like coming to live with us?" said Dewey.

"Yeah," said Ida, "that's it: like coming to live with you."

Mr. Sutton, slicing ham for Ellen to fry, said, "Have a seat and be company tonight. Ellen and I'll cook supper."

"Thank you kindly," said Ida, sitting down in the big rocking chair. The twins stood in front of her and watched as she rolled a cigarette. Randall sat on the rag rug near the fireplace and watched too. He knew what she would do next.

Ida stood up, struck a match on the seat of her riding pants, and lit the cigarette. Then she sat down again, dangled the bag of tobacco on one finger, and said, "Anybody care for a smoke?"

ABOUT THE AUTHOR

Robert Burch was born in Fayette County, Georgia, and grew up there with seven brothers and sisters. Despite the economic hardships of the 1930s, he relishes many happy memories of those years.

Mr. Burch draws on his childhood experiences for background material in his books, but, he says, "the incidents come from my imagination." Georgia is the setting for many of his popular books for young people, including *Queenie Peavy*, an ALA Notable Book; *Doodle and the Go-Cart; Hut School and the Wartime Home-Front Heroes;* and *Wilkin's Ghost*.

About *Ida Early Comes Over the Mountain*, Mr. Burch says, "I first thought of Ida more than ten years ago. I did a sketch of her then and relegated her to my subconscious. She kept reappearing until I knew that I must write more about her."

Although Mr. Burch still calls Georgia home, he says, "I admit to being something of a gypsy, having lived in Tokyo, London, and New York. Freighter travel interests me, and I have circled the globe, but in the years ahead I would like to travel extensively in my own country."

Mr. Burch is working on a new novel about Ida Early.